DEVON DELANEY SHOULD TOTALLY KNOW BETTER

By Lauren Barnholdt

ALADDIN M!X
NEW YORK   LONDON   TORONTO   SYDNEY

ALADDIN M!X

An imprint of Simon & Schuster Children's Publishing Division

1230 Avenue of the Americas, New York, NY 10020

First Aladdin M!X edition September 2009

Copyright © 2009 by Lauren Barnholdt

All rights reserved, including the right of reproduction in whole or in part in any form.

ALADDIN is a trademark of Simon & Schuster, Inc., and related logo is a registered trademark of Simon & Schuster, Inc.

ALADDIN M!X and related logo are registered trademarks of Simon & Schuster, Inc.

For information about special discounts for bulk purchases, please contact Simon & Schuster Special Sales at 1-866-506-1949 or business@simonandschuster.com.

The Simon & Schuster Speakers Bureau can bring authors to your live event. For more information or to book an event contact the Simon & Schuster Speakers Bureau at 1-866-248-3049 or visit our website at www.simonspeakers.com.

Designed by Tom Daly

The text of this book was set in Arrus.

Manufactured in the United States of America

10 9 8 7 6 5 4 3 2 1

Library of Congress Control Number 2009922830

ISBN 978-1-4169-8019-3

ISBN 978-1-4169-9679-8 (eBook)

For my grandparents,
Angeline and Charles Brauchle,
for their generosity, kindness,
and wonderful example

Thank you so, so, much to:

My amazing editor, **Kate Angelella,**
for her awesome suggestions, enthusiasm, and advice

My agent, **Alyssa Eisner Henkin,**
for always working tirelessly on my behalf

My **mom,** for always being there
My **sisters,** for being my best friends
My **dad** and **Beth,** for their support
Jodi Yanarella, Kevin Cregg, Scott Neumyer,
and the **Gorvine family** for their encouragement

Everyone who bought *The Secret Identity of Devon Delaney,*
and e-mailed me to tell me they loved it—thank you so
much for loving Devon as much as I do!
And last but not least, my husband, **Aaron,** for supporting me
no matter what, loving me no matter what, and making
me believe that anything is possible. . . .

chapter one

I think I have figured out the bane of my existence. The bane of one's existence, in case you don't already know, is the thing that is driving you the craziest. The thing that makes you absolutely totally nuts, the thing that if it did not exist, you could just relax and have a perfect life.

But the bane of my existence is not a thing. The bane of my existence is a person. And that person is Bailey Barelli.

Take right now, for example. Bailey Barelli is sitting one row over and three seats ahead of me in English. Which is fine. What is not fine, is that sitting in my row, and three seats up, is my boyfriend, Luke. Which means that Luke is sitting *right next to* Bailey Barelli.

Which would not be so bad, except two minutes ago, I saw her pass a note to Luke. Then I saw Luke open it, give Bailey a smile, and then write something on her note and *pass it back to her.* This is very unacceptable behavior, in my opinion. Plus, the bell has just rung. Which means all this unacceptable note passing started as soon as the bell rang, like she couldn't even wait one second. What was so important that she had to tell Luke, anyway? They're not even friends.

"Please everyone put your desks in a circle," our teacher, Mrs. Bancock, says. She grabs her grade book off her desk and walks to the front of the room. "We're going to get started."

I stand up and push my desk into the circle, right between Cassie Schafter and Michael Ronson. We're reading *Romeo and Juliet*, and Mrs. Bancock thinks we'll "absorb more Shakespeare" if we act out the parts. So every day, we put our desks in a circle, and spend the period reenacting *Romeo and Juliet*. Well, not actually reenacting. We just read out loud from our desks.

"Now," Mrs. Bancock says. She pushes her glasses up on her nose, and settles into a student desk at the head of the circle, her long skirt billowing around her.

"Today is my favorite day of *Romeo and Juliet*, because we are going to be reading the balcony scene. And," she goes on, "as a special treat, this time we will be acting out the action!"

A nervous laugh goes through the class. The balcony scene. That's the most famous scene of the play—where Romeo and Juliet declare their love for each other, and Romeo climbs up the balcony and I think he might even kiss Juliet. That could actually be kind of fun, since Romeo is played by Gabriel Warren, this slightly annoying guy in our class who has a Mohawk.

"I'm ready whenever you are," Bailey Barelli says, and flips her long, dark hair over one shoulder. Bailey Barelli is, of course, Juliet. This is because when Mrs. Bancock called for volunteers, Bailey Barelli shouted out, "I'LL DO IT!" really loud and raised her hand and was practically jumping out of her seat. You'd think teachers would be smart enough to realize that this kind of behavior is annoying and that whoever's doing it is obviously just sucking up, but they totally don't, since Mrs. Bancock just smiled and said, "Your enthusiasm is refreshing, Bailey. Let's put you down for the part of Juliet." Sigh.

I open my book to the balcony scene, and catch Luke's eye across the room, where he's sitting on the other side of the circle. He shoots me a smile, and I smile back before returning my eyes to my book. I'm still not exactly sure how I'm supposed to act around him. I mean, yeah, he is my boyfriend, but he's only been my boyfriend for two weeks.

And he's my first boyfriend. So it's not like I can say, *Oh, right, when my last boyfriend and I were going out for two weeks, this is how it was.*

"Oh, except," Bailey Barelli says, "Gabriel's not here." She reaches into her bag, pulls out a lip gloss, and smears some on her lips.

"Oh," Mrs. Bancock says. She looks around the room. "Well, I guess we'll need a replacement Romeo for the day." She peers over the top of her glasses. "Now, who would like to play Romeo? Of course you'll receive extra credit."

To my horror, I see Luke raise his hand on the other side of the room. What? Why? Is Luke crazy? Has he lost his mind? Does he not understand that when you have a girlfriend, you do not decide to be the Romeo to someone else's Juliet? I do my best to send him a look that says, *Why are you doing that, please put your hand down immediately.* But he doesn't seem to understand. I close my eyes and open them again, sure I have imagined this. But no. There he is, calmly sitting there with his hand in the air, like it's totally normal.

And then I think about how Bailey was just smearing that lip gloss all over her lips. So I do the only thing I can be expected to do in a situation like this. I pull a Bailey Barelli. "I'll do it!" I say, waving my hand around. "I'll play Romeo!"

Mrs. Bancock looks at me, surprised. I don't usually volunteer for things with such, uh, enthusiasm. And definitely not for something like playing Romeo. "Devon Delaney," she says. "*You* want to play Romeo?"

"Oh, yes, please," I tell her, nodding my head up and down furiously. "I really need the extra credit." This isn't really true. I mean, of course I could *use* the extra credit, but I'm not in trouble with the class or anything.

"Well," she says, "I don't see any reason why we have to be sexist! You shouldn't be discounted from getting the part just because you're a woman." And that's how I end up down on one knee, spending first period reenacting the balcony scene from Romeo and Juliet with Bailey Barelli.

Whatever. Luke probably just needed the extra credit. He's very smart, and always trying to do extra work.

It's one of the things I love about him. And passing notes is so not a big deal. I pass notes with people all the time. Besides, I'm a confident, mature woman. I'm not threatened just because Luke got passed a note by some other girl. I mean, he's waiting for *me* after class, not Bailey. He's going to be walking *me* to science class, not Bailey. He likes *me*, not Bailey. In fact, I'm sure he's going to tell me all about it. Including all the pertinent details, like why the note was passed, what was in it, why he wrote her back, etc. And then maybe he'll even talk about how annoying she is.

"Good job," Luke says as we walk.

"At what?" I ask. I'm weaving through the crowd of kids in the science wing, and it's taking all my strength not to trip in the new shoes I'm wearing. I got them at the consignment shop with my BFF, Lexi—totally cute, and black with a little heel. They're half a size too small, but they were five dollars! Pain is totally worth it for five dollars.

"At playing Romeo." Luke reaches through the throng of kids and takes my hand, and a rush of heat slides up my arm. I'm still not used to holding hands in public like this. Although I guess it's not really public. It's school. But still. People can see. Anyone could just be walking down the hall and go, "Oh, look, there's Devon holding hands with Luke."

"I never thought I'd be able to imagine you as a guy, but you really pulled it off." He shoots me a grin.

"Thanks," I say, a little uncertainly this time. What does he mean, he never saw me as a guy before? I mean, I'm flattered that he thinks I'm a good actress. (Actor?) But does Luke think of me as masculine now? That would be rather unfortunate, since I totally wore my cutest outfit today (black and gray dress over black ribbed tights, and the aforementioned new shoes).

"Well, here we are," I say, stopping outside of my science class. "Thanks for walking me to class." I give him an expectant look, waiting for him to mention the fact that he and Bailey were passing notes at the beginning of the period. Well, one note. That I saw.

"Yup, here we are," he says. He shifts his book bag from one shoulder to the other.

"Almost time for you to get to math," I remind him, in case he's forgotten that we're on a time schedule here.

"Yup," he agrees. "Almost time."

I practice putting an "I'm your girlfriend and you can tell me anything" kind of look on my face.

"Oh!" Luke says, "I almost forgot!"

Aha! I knew he would never keep anything from

me. Luke and I have a very honest relationship, one built on mutual trust and—

"I have to stay after tonight, for mock trial. But I'll give you a call later, when I get home." And then he squeezes my hand and takes off down the hall. Sigh. So much for honesty.

When I get into science, I slide into my seat next to my other BFF, Mel. She's looking at something in her binder, but quickly closes it when she sees me. "What are you looking at?" I ask.

"Nothing," she says quickly, but a guilty look passes over her face. "Just trying to get a head start on the reading."

"What reading?" I ask, feeling slightly panicked. "There was reading?"

"No, no," she says. "I just mean for next week." She takes her science book off the bottom of her pile of books and places it on top of her binder. "What's up?"

"Nothing," I sigh. "Except that I'm having a crisis."

"What sort?" Mel asks, her brown eyes serious.

"A boyfriend crisis," I announce. I lean in close so that no one will overhear. Some of Luke's friends from soccer sit at the lab table behind us, and the last thing I need is them reporting back to Luke about my obvious insecurity. "Luke was passing notes with Bailey Barelli during English, and to stop it, I had to play Romeo to her Juliet." I pause and wait for Mel to exclaim how horrible that is.

But all she says is, "What kind of notes?"

"I dunno," I say. "That's the point. He didn't tell me what it said."

"Wait, notes or note?" Mel asks.

"Note," I say. "Well, that I saw anyway." I think about it. "Is there any way they could have been discussing class work over more than one note?" You'd think one note would be enough. One note I'm willing to forgive. Two notes, now that's a little more serious.

"Devon," Mel says, in a tone that makes me think I'm not going to really like what she has to say. "Maybe you should just trust Luke. It could have been anything in those notes." I look at her skeptically. "And," she rushes on. "If you're worried about it, maybe you should just ask him." There's a pause, and then Mel says, "Remember how being honest and straightforward is the best policy?"

I shift uncomfortably in my seat. I know she's thinking about a little, uh, *situation* I had a few weeks ago. See, this summer I stayed with my grandma while my parents were sorting out some problems in their marriage, and while I was there, I met this girl named Lexi Cortland. I kind of sort of accidentally might have told Lexi that at my school back home, I was totally popular and dating Jared Bentley, the most popular guy at Robert Hawk Junior High. Which wasn't true, but I figured it was summer, I was just having fun, and I'd never see Lexi again.

Except then Lexi transferred to my school last month, and I had to spend a lot of time and energy scrambling around trying to fix everything. It all became super complicated, because I was trying to pretend Jared was my boyfriend, even though he wasn't, and then I started liking Luke, and Jared starting liking Lexi. And to make matters worse, Luke and Jared are best friends. It was all a very tangled mess.

"But that all turned out fine," I remind Mel, waving my hand like it was no big deal. And it did. Lexi and I are now BFF, she's going out with Jared, and Luke and I are together. And yes, there were some, um, challenges to be worked out, but everything's fine now. Better than fine, in fact.

"Helllllllo," Lexi trills, walking into the classroom and sliding down on the other side of the table. "How are my girls this lovely morning?"

Lexi's a morning person, probably because she gets a cappuccino every morning on her way to school. Lexi doesn't ride the bus. Her mom drives her in, and they stop at Starbucks.

"Not so well," I say. "I just had to play Romeo to Bailey Barelli's Juliet."

"Ugh, *Barelli*," Lexi says, wrinkling up her small nose to show her distaste. "I'm so not a fan."

"Thank you!" I say, throwing my hands up in the air. I give Mel a "see? she is pretty bad and I'm not overreacting" kind of look.

"Well, I have news, too," Lexi says. She folds her hands on the table and waits. I notice that her nails are painted light blue with little silvery star stickers on them. Very cute. Mel and I look at her expectantly. "Aren't you going to ask me what it is?"

"What is it?" Mel asks.

"Jared asked me to the dance." We all squeal, even though since Jared is Lexi's boyfriend, it's kind of a given that he would ask her to the dance. But still. It's a semiformal, which is kind of a big deal.

"Has Luke asked you yet?" Lexi asks. "We all have to go together."

"No," I say, grabbing the frayed corner of my science notebook and scratching it with my fingernail.

"And even if he does, the real problem is going to be getting my mom to allow me to go with him."

"Well, you better start working on her now," Lexi says wisely.

Hmmm. Good point. Maybe I can offer to do some more chores around the house? And then she'll be all, "Devon, you have been so amazing lately, of course you can go to the dance."

"Yeah," Mel says. "Your mom's the type that's going to need a *lot* of work. More than just doing chores around the house or something."

Great.

chapter two

Later that night. Dinner. My mom is at the stove, making something in a big pot, and I am at the table, doing my homework. Every so often, I'll ask her a question, like, "How do you spell 'necessary'?" or "What's the capital of North Dakota?" This all has nothing to do with my homework, and everything to do with preparing for my big request, which is, you know, that I'm allowed to go to the dance.

My plan is that if I appear like I need instruction and guidance, she will assume that the dance is a very innocent endeavor. Plus, I'm going to tell her I'm going with a group of friends. Which isn't exactly a lie. Lexi and Jared are my friends, and Luke was my friend before he was my boyfriend. Well, sort of. We were friends for like a week or two. But still. It counts.

"Look at my picture, Devon!" my sister Katie instructs. She shoves the piece of construction paper she's been scribbling on in my face.

"What is it?" I ask, frowning. It looks likes two stick figures with big yellow dots on their chests.

"It's my homework," Katie says solemnly, even though she's in preschool and doesn't get any homework. "It's a picture."

"Yes," I say. "But what is it a picture *of*?" Then I remember that I'm not supposed to ask Katie what her pictures are of, since that makes it seem like I can't tell. Which I can't, but I don't want to make her feel bad. Katie's only five, and she's still getting over the fact that we had to go stay with my grandmother this summer. My mom and dad call it "a difficult transition." A lot of times I want to point out that I'm having a difficult transition, too, since over the summer my parents basically bought me everything I wanted, because they felt guilty, and now that they don't, I'm stuck wearing all my old clothes. "I mean," I correct, "please tell me about your picture."

"Well," she says. "It's you and me getting Olympic medals." She points at the page. "See? There's me, getting the gold, and there's you, getting the bronze." She reaches over and pats my hand. "Don't worry," she says. "Better luck next time."

"Thanks," I say, resisting the urge to roll my eyes at her. I stare closely at the paper. "What are those things on my face?" There are little red dots on my cheeks, and pink and purple smudges all around my eyes.

"That's your makeup," Katie explains. She selects a blue crayon and adds a layer of eye shadow.

"I wear makeup to the Olympics?"

"Yes," she says solemnly. "The Olympics are on national television. You know that, don't you, Devon?"

"Yes, of course I know that," I say. "But how come you're not wearing makeup then?"

"Because I'm not old enough." She puts her crayon back.

"That's right," my mom says from the stove. She's frowning at a recipe that she's printed off the internet. My mom's new thing is watching the Food Network, then printing off her fave recipes to try. Rachael Ray is like her new best friend. "You're not old enough to wear makeup, Katie."

"But when I'm thirteen like Devon, I can wear it," Katie reports.

"Not to school," my mom says. She stirs whatever's in the pot. "You can't wear makeup to school until you're sixteen."

This is definitely not the way I want the conversation to go, with my mom listing things that aren't age appropriate right before I'm about to ask her about the dance. I decide I need to seize control of the situation.

"But," I say. "Katie, you *will* be able to wear makeup to other things. Like, for example, if you want to go to the mall with your friends." Which my mom lets me do. All the time. "Or if you want to have fun at a sleepover." Again, totally allowed. "Or if you want to go to a semiformal at school or something." My mom's nodding her head at the stove, but at the mention of the word "semiformal," her forehead wrinkles up.

"Well, Katie," she says. "You don't need to be worried about going to any dances anytime soon. Those are only for big girls."

"Right," I agree. "Like when you're my age."

Katie jumps out of her chair. "Sometimes we do the chicken dance at school. And it goes like this. 'With a little bit of this and a little bit of that and shake, shake, shake!'" She shakes around. "So I am old enough to go to dances."

"No," my mom says. "You're not. Dances are for big girls."

"I am a big girl!" Katie says. Uh-oh. I can sense a tantrum coming on. And when Katie has a tantrum, it's not good for anyone. Especially my mom, because she will not be in a good, let-Devon-go-to-the-dance kind of mood.

"Katherine Delaney, you will not—" my mom starts.

But at that moment, the back door opens and my dad comes sliding into the kitchen, home from work. "Something smells good in here!" he says, sounding relieved. It actually does smell good in here. Like tomatoes and some kind of meat. I hope it's goulash.

"What are you making?" I ask. My mom isn't exactly the best cook.

"She's making food that is hot, hot, hot on your tongue!" Katie reports. She's sitting back at the table now, her tantrum forgotten for the moment.

"It's not that hot," my mom says. "It's a chicken tikka masala, a traditional Indian dish."

"I love chicken tikka masala," my dad says, setting

his briefcase down and giving my mom a kiss on the cheek. "We used to always order it from that little Indian place down the street from our first apartment, do you remember that?"

"Yes, and we ordered from there so much that they got to know our order before we'd even tell them." My mom gets a dreamy look on her face. Ugh. I feel a little disgusted, because let's face it, it's kind of gross to see your parents being all in love with each other. Although I am happy they're getting along.

My parents have been in counseling lately, in order to get through their "marital roadblocks and issues." I definitely think this past summer of me and Katie being away worked out well. For them, anyway. I mean, there was that whole tricky business about me making up a whole fake life for myself.

The phone rings, and my dad gets to it first, before Katie can jump out of her chair. "Devon, it's Luke," he says, handing me the phone.

Ooh, yay! Maybe he's calling to ask me to the dance! Or to tell me all about his note-passing with Bailey, and how it didn't mean anything. My mom and dad give each other a look: one of those "There's a boy calling our house for Devon and how do we feel about that?" kind of looks.

"Hi, Luke," I say, stretching the phone cord as far as it will go, through the archway of the kitchen and into the living room. Honestly, there is no privacy in this house. The only cordless is upstairs in my parents' room. I don't even have a cell phone, like everyone else my age. My mom thinks it's "not necessary." Not necessary! Doesn't she know that cell phones save lives all the time? What if I get kidnapped, and I need a cell to text to the police where I am, so they can come and save me? It happens, I saw it on an episode of *Dateline*.

"Hey," Luke says, sounding cute and a little nervous. He always gets nervous when my dad answers the phone. I guess he doesn't realize that if he should be afraid of anyone around here, it's my mom.

"What's up?" My stomach flips. Luke and I talk on the phone almost every night, but like the hand-holding-in-the-halls thing, I'm still not completely used to it.

"Not much," he says. "Just got home from the first meeting of mock trial."

"Oh," I say. "Was it fun?"

"It was awesome," he says. Which I find hard to believe. In mock trial, kids get dressed up like judges and then reenact trials. I think. Or maybe they act out new, fake trials? Do they make them up? Who writes them? And why would you want to act out a trial?

"That's great," I say.

"Yeah, I'm going to be super busy with it," he says. "But it's good, you know? Now that soccer's over, I'm going to need something to occupy my time."

"Right," I say, wondering why he wouldn't want to occupy his time with me.

"So, listen," he says. "I've been meaning to ask you something."

"Oh, really?" I say innocently. "What about?"

Beep. The call waiting beeps on the other line. I check the caller ID, since my parents get super annoyed if I don't answer call waiting beeps when I'm on the phone. They're afraid they're going to miss important calls. Which is ridiculous, because if there was an important call that couldn't get through to the house phone, whoever it was could just call their cells. Unlike if the call is for me, because, hello, I don't have a cell. Beep. It's Lexi. I decide to call her back in a few minutes, when I can tell her the details of Luke asking me to the dance. Quietly of course, so that my parents don't overhear until I have a chance to ask them.

"Is that your call waiting?" Luke asks.

"No," I say. "Why?"

"Because it sounds like it's your call waiting. Your voice keeps cutting out."

Beep. Call waiting beeps again. I check the ID. Dr. Lucy Meyerson. My mom and dad's counselor. Crap, crap, crap. "Luke, can you hold on for one second?" I ask sweetly.

"Hello?" I answer the other line.

"Yes, hello, this is Dr. Meyerson's office calling to confirm the appointment for John and Marcia Delaney tomorrow at five o'clock?"

"Yes," I say, making a mental note to remind my parents at dinner. "They'll be there."

"And to whom am I speaking to, please?" the secretary asks, kind of snotty.

"Um, this is their daughter, Devon, and I would be happy to pass that message right along." I infuse my voice with the right amount of responsibility, and maybe a little bit of sadness. I mean, my parents are basically fine, but she doesn't need to know that. Maybe she'll be a little nicer to me if she thinks I'm very worried about them.

"Yes, well, I'd like to speak with your mommy or daddy. Are they available?"

Mommy or Daddy? Does she know I'm thirteen and on the other line with my maybe possibly very first dance date ever? "Well, they're not really available, per se," I tell her. Which is true. My mom is making dinner, and my dad is . . . um, helping her. Plus the phone isn't *technically* available, since I'm on the other line. "But like I said, I will be sure to give them the message." I look around for a piece of paper and a pen, but I don't see one. I hold the receiver up to the sweater I'm wearing and scratch my sleeve. "See? Writing it down."

"Thank you very much, Miss Delaney," she says, "but—"

"Please, call me Devon."

"Uh, Devon. But unfortunately I have a note here that says messages are not to be left with the children."

"Oh," I tell her. "They probably meant my little sister, Katie. She's five, and horrible with messages. One time it took her two days to tell me my friend Mel called."

"Well, it doesn't just say Katie," she says. "It says here that—"

"Okay, fine," I say. "Just hold on one second." It's obvious that I'm going to have to tell Luke to hold on, give the phone to my mom, and have her talk to this crazy woman.

I push the button to click over. "Luke? Can you hold on for like one more sec? It's for my mom, but it'll be quick."

"Sorry," the same annoying secretary says. "It's still me."

Must not have pushed the button all the way. I try again. "Luke?"

"Nope." Again.

"Hello, Luke?"

"No, still me. Maybe he hung up?" she offers helpfully.

Ugh.

I call my dad to the phone, since my mom is now at the stove, peering into the pot and saying, "I'm not sure it's supposed to be this color."

"It's okay, Mommy," Katie says, patting her arm. "I wanted pizza anyway."

I come back into the kitchen and plop back down in front of my homework. Why would Luke hang up right before he was going to ask me to the dance? Did he have another call, too? Did his mom call him to dinner? Did he get so nervous that he needed some more time to collect his thoughts?

"Try this," my mom says, holding a bowl out to me. In the bottom is a small spoonful of what looks like red slime, over a hard bump. "What's that bumpy thing?" I ask.

"Chicken," she says. She pulls a paper towel off the roll and uses it to wipe a small spot of tomato sauce off her forehead.

"I want to try it, I want to try it!" Katie sings, dancing around.

"Okay," I say. She grabs two forks from the drawer, and I use one of them to cut the piece of chicken in half. Katie spears one, and I spear the other. "Blow on it first," I tell her. "So that it's not too hot." Katie blows on her chicken obediently.

"Now keep in mind that it's going to be over rice," my mom says, as if that will change the entire taste of what I'm about to put in my mouth. She gives the box of Minute rice that's sitting on the counter a shake. She looks nervous.

"This isn't going to give me food poisoning or anything, is it?" I ask.

"Devon! No, it's not going to give you food poisoning!"

"This is poison?" Katie looks worried.

"No," I say. "It's fine. Ready?" She nods. "One, two, three!" We both pop the food into our mouths at the same time and chew. It tastes exactly like it looks—

like rubbery chicken in tomato sauce, but with some sort of weird spices.

"Well," I say, after I swallow. "It's not bad exactly." My mom's face falls. "But I'm sure it will be better after the rice."

"Excuse me, please," Katie says, her mouth full. And then she leans over the bowl and spits her chicken back in. "But I don't really like that, thank you very much."

"What don't you like, Katie-bug?" my dad asks, returning the phone to its cradle.

"Did anyone call for me?" I ask hopefully, thinking maybe Luke called back. But my dad shakes his head.

"The Indian is a disaster," my mom says. She laughs and grabs the pizza menu out of the drawer by the fridge.

"Ooh, I want extra cheese on mine," I say. Delish.

"Me too," Katie says, just to copy me.

"John?" my mom asks. "What do you want on your pizza?"

"So we're just going to throw this out?" my dad asks, looking at the big pot of disgustingness that's on the stove. "After we spent all that money on Indian spices?"

My mom tightens her mouth into a hard line. "Well," she says. "Do *you* want to try to make the tikka masala?" She unties her apron and holds it out to my dad. "The girls and I will just go and watch a movie, and you can call us when it's ready."

"Mommy," Katie says, wagging her finger. "You're using harsh tones."

Harsh tones are something my mom and dad are working with their therapist on. Basically it means that when you get upset, you have to do your best not to express your dismay in harsh tones. You just convey how you feel with words. I think it's all well and good for my parents to be working on their harsh tones, but Katie is like the Harsh Tones Police.

"I'm sorry," my dad says. "I wasn't trying to imply that I was mad about the dinner. Of course we can order pizza."

"And I'm sorry if I got defensive," my mom says. "I just was disappointed that the dinner didn't turn out right, and it felt like you were criticizing me."

Katie claps her hands. "No harsh tones! No harsh tones!" she sings, dancing around the kitchen.

The phone rings. Yay! Must be Luke, calling me back. "I'll get it!" I cry, rushing over to the receiver to check the caller ID. Oh. Lexi. Again.

"Hey, Lex," I say. "I can't talk long, we're about to eat dinner."

"Okay," she says, sounding nervous. Lexi never sounds nervous. Ever. Even a few weeks ago, when she and Kim Cavalli, the most popular girl in seventh grade, got into a fight over this guy Matt Connors. Lexi didn't even care when it almost came to blows in the hallway at school. She was the picture of calm. Okay, maybe not the picture of calm, but she was pretty calm for the situation.

"What's up?"

"Well," she says. "I don't mean to upset you or anything, especially because of that whole thing in science today."

"What whole thing in science?"

"The thing about Bailey Barelli, and how she's the bane of your existence."

"Oh, that," I say. Out of the corner of my eye, I can see my mom ordering the pizza from her cell phone. "That was just a temporary bout of insanity. In fact, I'm totally over it. I'm sure it was nothing. Besides, Luke called me when he got home from mock trial, and he was totally about to ask me to the dance." I lower my voice when I say that last part, just in case.

"He was?" Lexi squeals. "Ohmigod, that is amazing! We can all go together, just like I said! We can probably get my mom to bring us in the Hummer!" Lexi's mom bought a Hummer last week. It's this huge car that pretty much looks ridiculous, but I guess Mrs. Cortland must have really wanted it, because they're super expensive. My mom says Lexi's mom must not care too much about the environment, since those cars are horrible on gas. "That does sound fun," I say, starting to get excited. "I just have to ask my parents first." I look into the kitchen, wondering if now's the time. Maybe I should wait until they're all full of pizza and in a carb coma.

"Oh, I'm so glad he's going to ask you," Lexi says. She lowers her voice. "Actually, Devi, I was worried about telling you this, but now that I know it's okay, I'll tell you."

"What?" I ask.

"Wellll," she says. "I just got off the phone with Jared, and he just got off the phone with Luke."

"Wait, Jared just got off the phone with Luke?"

"Yeah, and then he called me. Jared, not Luke." My head is spinning, trying to keep track of all the calls. This would be so much easier if I could just text like a normal person. "Anyway," Lexi goes on. "Jared said that Luke had a really fun time at mock trial."

"I know," I say. "He told me." Who cares that Luke had a fun time at mock trial? The more important thing here is that Luke obviously hung up on me and then called Jared. How rude! He should have called me back immediately. Oh, wait. That's not right. Because Lexi was beeping in while I was on the phone with Luke. I relax. But then I realize that means that Luke must have called Jared *before* he called me. Hmm. I'm not sure which is worse.

"Wellll," Lexi says again.

"Lexi," I instruct. "Spit it out." Honestly, the girl is killing me.

"Bailey Barelli is in mock trial."

"Oh. Well. Whatever. I mean, I can't stop her from signing up for some extracurricular activity. Besides, I told you, I'm not worried."

And then Lexi decides to drop a bombshell. "Devi, you're so awesome!" she says. "I would be freaking out if Jared was doing something with one of his ex-girlfriends."

"What do you mean, ex-girlfriend?" I frown at this new bit of information.

"Barelli is Luke's ex-girlfriend," Lexi tells me.

"What do you mean, his ex-girlfriend?" I repeat. Obviously, this is some kind of mistake. Luke doesn't have an ex-girlfriend. I'm his first girlfriend. Just like he's my first boyfriend.

"They dated last year," Lexi explains, "Oh, God, Devi, I thought you knew."

The doorbell rings. "Devon!" my mom calls from the kitchen. "Can you get that? It must be the pizza." Already? What are they, Speed Demon Pizza?

I consider yelling back that I'm busy, but then realize if I want to portray myself as the sensible, responsible daughter who is allowed to go to the dance, then I should probably go get the pizza. I sigh. "I gotta go," I say to Lexi. "We'll talk about this later."

I go to the door to get the pizza, even though I'm not sure I'm hungry anymore. An ex-girlfriend he never even mentioned? This makes his note-passing even more unacceptable. But how to handle this? Ask him? Ignore it? Get it out of him in some roundabout way?

When I get back to the kitchen, pizza in hand, my mom's at the computer in the corner. Probably doing work stuff. My mom quit her job to pursue her dream of a freelance web design career, so she works any chance she gets.

"Where're Dad and Katie?" I ask.

"They'll be down in a second," my mom says, clicking away.

"Mom," I say, deciding to seize the opportunity of having my mom alone. "What would you do if you thought that maybe the guy you liked might like someone else? Or that he used to date someone else, but he wasn't telling you?" I'm very careful not to use the word "boyfriend" since my mom doesn't *exactly* know that I have one. A boyfriend, I mean.

My mom frowns, and her eyebrows crinkle in the middle. "You mean like he lied to you?"

"Not exactly lied," I say. I grab some plates from the cupboard and start setting the table. "But just . . . didn't mention it."

"Lying by omission is still lying," my mom says ominously. She gets this certain serious look on her face, which probably means she's quoting something she learned in therapy.

"So you think I, um, that this person should be mad?"

"Devon," she says, "Come here." I walk over to her.

"You," she says, "are amazing and perfect and any guy who can't see that, or who is going to lie to you by omission, is not worth it."

I sigh. She has to say that. She's my mom. Plus she doesn't exactly know the whole situation, that Luke is my boyfriend. But . . . I start to think about it. Maybe she's right. I mean, Luke's with me now. Not Bailey. And besides, what does Bailey have that I don't have? Who cares if she has a key chain that says Italian Princess in sparkly letters and long tumbling dark hair and smoky eyes? Anyone can buy a keychain. And anyone can get smoky eyes with a little bit of help from some eye shadow. (Well, anyone whose mom lets her wear eye shadow.)

I start to feel better. I'm much better than Bailey Barelli. Who cares if she's cute but also tomboyish and is a great athlete and is in stupid mock trial? I played intramural soccer when I was in fifth grade, and I could join mock trial if I wanted.

"Oh, honey, you didn't tell me you played a part in English today," my mom says happily.

"What?" I ask. "How did you know about that?" I look over her shoulder at the computer screen. She's logged onto Mrs. Bancock's website, where there's a section where parents can click to see what's going on in our English class, along with a section to check our grades, etc. Sometimes Mrs. Bancock even puts up pictures. And right there, in the middle of the website, is a picture of me this morning in English.

Bailey Barelli is standing on Mrs. Bancock's desk, her long curly hair like a halo around her face, and her smoky eyelids lowered. I'm on the ground, down on one knee, and whoever took the picture (probably Mrs. Bancock—I was so worried about what I looked like, that I must not have noticed she was playing photographer) snapped it in the middle of me saying a line. My mouth is half open, and since I'm down on my knee, I'm off balance and almost falling over. Not the most flattering pic.

"Why are you down on your knee, honey?" my mom asks, peering at the screen. "And who is that girl? She looks like she's about seventeen!"

Sigh. So much for beating Barelli.

chapter three

Whatever. I'm not thinking about it. I am an independent woman, who does not need to be insecure about my relationship with Luke. So what if he never called me back last night? I am way above waiting by the phone for a guy. Which I totally didn't. And fine, maybe there was a little bit of waiting by the computer for him to IM me (which he never did), but I would have been on the computer anyway. Chatting with friends, googling my hobbies and interests, doing things online that people do when they're busy and important.

"Hey," Mel says, coming up behind me in study hall the next day.

"Hey," I say, turning around, happy to see her. She slides into the chair across from me.

"Do you want to maybe stay after school with me today?" she asks. "It's the first meeting for radio."

Our school recently announced that they're going to be starting a school radio station. It's actually pretty cool—we're going to have a studio on campus and everything, and we're going to be featuring original programming all throughout the day. Some music, but mostly school news and talk shows. The best part? We're allowed to listen to it in study halls and the library during our free periods. How cool is that? And they're going to play it over the loudspeaker between classes.

"Definitely," I say. "I just have to call my mom." Which means I'm going to have to borrow Lexi's cell phone. Honestly, this whole not-having-a-phone thing is getting to be a bit ridiculous.

"Hey, did you know that Luke and Bailey Barelli used to go out?" I ask Mel, hoping I sound nonchalant. I scratch my pencil on my math homework, pretending I'm working on a problem.

"Yeah," she says. "Last year, right?"

"Yeah," I say. "How come I didn't know this?" And how come everybody else did? Was there some kind of big announcement last year, like, "Hey, everyone, Bailey and Luke are dating! Yay!" Or even worse, maybe they were one of those super annoying couples who are always holding hands and kissing in the hallways. I mean, Luke and I hold hands. But not all the time. Maybe we need to bump it up a bit. Does everyone know Luke and *I* are dating?

"Because last year you were more concerned about Jared Bentley than about Luke." Mel reaches into her bag and pulls out her science book, and sets it down on the table in front of us.

"Oh," I say. "Right." This makes sense. Last year I *was* totally obsessed with Jared. I mean, obviously, since I told Lexi he was my boyfriend. Of course, this was when I thought I'd never see Lexi again, but still. Then after I got to know Jared I realized he's . . . um . . . not the sharpest tool in the shed. And I started liking Luke. But apparently while I was thinking about Jared, Luke was thinking about Bailey. The thought makes me stomach flip.

"How come you didn't say anything to me?" I ask Mel.

She shrugs. "I thought you knew."

Right.

At lunch, I take my seat at the A-list table with

Lexi, Luke, Jared, Kim Cavalli, and apparently Bailey. Bailey never used to really sit with us, but now that she and Kim have suddenly become BFF, she does. And Mel's usually here as well, but she had some sort of meeting in guidance. She got all secretive when I asked her what it was about. Probably she's getting some kind of award or something, and she's embarrassed. Mel gets like that anytime anyone notices how smart she is.

"Hey," I say, setting my tray down next to Luke's. "You weren't in English today."

"Dentist appointment," he says. He picks up the pizza on his tray and takes a bite. "You want some?" He holds it out to me. I don't really want any, since the cafeteria pizza is kind of gross. But out of the corner of my eye, I see Bailey watching me from the other side of Luke. And so I take a bite.

"That's good," I say. I pick up the napkin off Luke's tray and wipe a stray piece of cheese off my chin. Sharing pizza and napkins with my boyfriend! That's basically like kissing him in front of everyone.

"So anyway, Luke," Bailey says from the other side of him. "I just think the *Hamm v. The Board of Education* case is going to be so interesting. Seriously, we have to do it."

What is this "we" she's talking about? She's not a "we" with Luke. Me and Luke are a "we." I wish I could chime in with, *Hey, Luke, what are we doing about the dance?* but of course I can't because he hasn't asked me yet.

"I agree," Luke says. "It really is an interesting case, and I think there's so much we can do with it." See? Starting with a "we" can only lead to bad things. Now Luke's saying it, too.

"What's the case about?" I ask.

"I was going to tell you about it on the phone last night," Luke starts. Ha! Take that, Barelli! Luke and I were talking on the phone all last night. Well, until he forgot to call me back. He holds out the pizza and I take another bite. "It's really interesting, about this kid who didn't get into college because his principal—"

"It's actually way too complicated to get into here," Bailey says quickly, cutting him off. "But mock trial is seriously amazing, I have a feeling we're all going to have a lot of fun this year." She looks at Luke and gives him a big grin.

Oh, puhleeze. Amazing? Finding shoes for five dollars, maybe. Your fave show on TV after a long day, definitely. But mock trial? I think not. She's totally just trying to rub in my face how she's going to be having fun with my boyfriend.

"Well, maybe I'll join," I say suddenly, before I can stop myself.

"You will?" Luke looks surprised. I can't tell if he's happy surprised or not-happy surprised.

"Yeah," I say. "Why not? It sounds fun." My mom's always telling me I need to sign up for some extracurriculars. I'm already doing radio, so why not go for both? And the way these two are going on and on about it, maybe it really is fun. Just as long as I don't have to dress up like a judge or anything.

"You totally should," Barelli says, but I see the look of annoyance that briefly passes over her face.

"I think I will," I say. I glance down the table to where Lexi's sitting with Jared. She catches my eye and mouths, *Did he ask you yet?*

No, I mouth back. *But soon*. She smiles and gives me a thumbs up.

He *will* ask me soon. He was just about to on the phone last night. And besides, he's sharing his pizza with me. I mean, hello!

"Hey," Bailey says. "Can I have a bite of that?"

And then I realize she's looking at Luke's pizza! She wants Luke's pizza!

Doesn't she know that you don't share pizza with people you're not going out with?

"Sure," Luke says. He breaks a piece of pizza off for her. Ha! I knew Luke would never let her just take a bite. That's reserved for girlfriends only, thank you very much. But the next thing I know, Bailey leans over and eats the pizza right out of Luke's hand! Ohmigod. It is like he is FEEDING HER. My boyfriend is feeding Bailey Barelli pizza in front of everyone!

Her long dark hair brushes against his arm as she straightens up. "Mmm," she says, licking her lips. "Good." And then she smirks.

"But you said you wanted to join radio," Mel says, frowning.

"I know," I say. "But Luke was going on and on about how fun mock trial is, and I just figured that I could do both." The last bell just rang, and I'm at Mel's locker.

"But you *can't* do both," Mel says. "They meet on the same day." She finishes loading her books into her bag and slams her locker door shut.

"Then I guess I can't do radio."

Someone taps me on the shoulder. I turn around to find Jared Bentley standing there with a concerned look on his face. Up until a few weeks ago, if I'd turned around to see Jared Bentley standing behind me, I would have maybe fainted or freaked out. This is because I used to have a huge major crush on him. But now I'm just annoyed.

"Can I talk to you?" Jared asks. His eyes are serious.

"Um, sure," I say.

"Wait a minute," Mel says, slinging her bag over her shoulder and putting her hand on her hip. "Is this about Bailey?"

"Barelli?" Jared's interested, like he's about to get some good gossip.

"No," I say, shooting Mel a look that hopefully lets her know to keep her mouth shut about all of this in front of Jared.

"No, what?" Jared asks. He frowns.

"No, we weren't talking about Barelli," I say.

"But Mel just said 'Is this about Bailey?'" Jared reports.

"No, she didn't," I say, turning back around. "Did you, Mel?"

"I didn't," Mel says, sighing. "I said 'Is this about Hailey?'"

"Oh," Jared says, nodding. "Who's Hailey?"

"This girl I used to know," I tell him. "Anyway, uh, Mel, I'll catch up with you later? Meet me after radio?"

"Sure," Mel says, and takes off down the hall. She doesn't seem too happy with me. Not that I can blame her. I'd be annoyed, too, if she told me she was going to join something with me and then just changed her mind because of some guy. Although it's not really about a guy, per se. It's more about a girl. And not just any girl. An ex-girl*friend*. Totally admissible.

"What did you want to talk to me about?" I ask Jared, checking my watch. Two-thirty-three. Mock trial starts at two-forty, which means I have seven minutes to find out what Jared wants, reapply my lip gloss and brush my hair in the bathroom, and get to mock trial.

"Well, it's just that I saw what you were doing at lunch today," he says.

I start walking down the hall toward the girls' room, and he follows me. This is crazy. Jared Bentley following me down the hall. Me, joining mock trial to keep an eye on Luke. If you'd have told me four weeks ago this would be my life, I never would have believed you.

"What do you mean what I was doing at lunch today?" Is he going to bring up about how I was eating Luke's pizza and so was Bailey? Does Jared know something I don't? I decide maybe I should be a little nicer to him, since he might be a wealth of information.

"You know, the looks you were giving me, and how

you were trying to mouth me a secret message." He kicks at a wadded up piece of paper that someone left in the hall.

"What are you talking about?" I ask. And then I remember looking at Lexi and mouthing to her about Luke not asking me to the dance yet. Jared was sitting right next to her, and he must have thought I was talking to him. "Oh, that," I say. "I was trying to talk to Lexi."

"Devi, it's okay," he says. We're outside the girls' bathroom now, and so I stop. He puts his hand on my shoulder. "Just because you're dating Luke and I'm going out with Lexi doesn't mean that I just expect you to lose all your feelings for me just like that." He snaps his fingers, I guess to symbolize how quickly he doesn't expect me to lose my feelings for him, and then he pats my shoulder in a "it's okay that you like me and I'm not interested" kind of way.

Oh, geez. I cannot believe this. Jared Bentley thinks I still like him. I try to figure out what to say without being mean. "Well," I say slowly. "While it is true that I used like you, uh, now I like Luke. Luke is my boy-friend." He looks at me blankly. "I'm going out with LUKE." I say the last part real slow.

"So you don't like me?" Jared tries. A look of wonder crosses his face, like he can't really fathom the idea that any girl might not like him. I can't really blame him. Most girls do.

"Not anymore."

"Oh, good," he says. His face breaks out into a relieved grin. Well. He doesn't have to look so happy about it. Would it be the end of the world if I liked him? He squeezes my shoulder. "Well, I guess I'll see you in mock trial."

"You're in mock trial?" I ask, surprised. He doesn't seem like the type.

"Lexi made me join," he says gloomily.

"Oh, right." I convinced Lexi to join during seventh period. Apparently it took all of eighth and ninth for Lexi to recruit Jared as well. How is this fair? While I'm wandering around, trying to figure out why Luke is passing notes with some other girl, Lexi is choosing her boyfriend's extracurricular activities.

Jared continues down the hall, and I duck into the bathroom. I pull my lip gloss out of my purse and regloss my lips. My lip gloss is called, "SHOW HIM YOU CAN." That sounds highly inappropriate. Although maybe the person who came up with it meant "Show him you can forget about Barelli and kick butt at mock trial."

I run a brush through my hair, and then reach into

my purse and pull out my bronzer, which I brush onto my cheeks, leaving myself glowy and bronze. I smile at myself in the mirror. From the stalls, the sound of feet shuffling comes, and then a voice.

"He *is* really cute," the voice says, and I freeze. It's Kim Cavalli, aka Bailey Barelli's new BFF, aka my archenemy. Kim's pretty much the most popular girl in school (although Lexi's close to taking over that title), and Lexi actually liked her when she first got to our school. But then Kim stole this guy Lexi used to like away from her (Matt Connors), and then told everyone that I lied about dating Jared. Kim actually used to like Luke, too. The whole thing is very scandalous.

"He is sooo cute," another voice says, and I realize it's Barelli. Bailey Barelli and Kim Cavalli are having a personal, private conversation, and I'm eavesdropping. I slide my lip gloss slowly back into my purse and curse myself for wearing shoes that make so much noise. "I just wish he didn't have to be so smart," Bailey continues, giggling. "I mean, come on, mock trial? Now I have to give up my whole afternoon just to reenact trials that aren't even real."

"I know," Kim sighs. "Lame. That's one of the reasons my crush on him only lasted about five minutes."

"I really have a feeling we're going to be getting back together soon," Bailey says.

"Totally," Kim agrees. "Come on, *Devon Delaney*?"

They both giggle, like it's the craziest thing they've ever head, and then the sound of a toilet flushing fills the room. I run out before they can figure out that I've been listening. Ohmigod, ohmigod, ohmigod. She does want him back! And she totally joined mock trial just because Luke did! How ridiculous and lame! Joining something just because a guy you like joins is an insult to feminism everywhere. These kinds of things are exactly what our great grandmothers fought against when—oh. Wait a minute. I'm doing the same thing. But that's different. Luke's my boyfriend. And I'm just keeping an eye on him.

Bailey and Kim come out of the bathroom and breeze by me in a haze of perfume. When they're a few feet down the hall, Bailey looks back at me, leans in and whispers something to Kim, and then they both laugh before disappearing into the room where mock trial is going to be held.

"Hey," Lexi says from behind me, and I jump. "What's with you?"

"Nothing," I say, squaring my shoulders as we head for mock trial. "Just war."

@ @ @

Twenty minutes later. Mock trial. We have been sepa-
rated into groups of four, and we're supposed to be
going over a case that's been given to us. I thought
it would be more like acting, but apparently a lot of
it has to do with the Constitution. I'm all about the
Constitution—freedom, yay!—but this might be taking it a little too far.

The faculty advisor, Mr. Ikwang, is one of those
teachers that's super excited about the judicial process.
Those were his words, not mine. "I'm super excited
about the judicial process, and I hope you will be too!"
he said as soon as we got into the room.

Snore.

In my group are Lexi, Jared, and Luke. Lexi took
control of the situation when Mr. Ikwang told us to
get into groups, announcing, "Jared and Luke, you'll be
with me and Devon."

Then she grabbed my hand and pulled me over to
their table, where we're now all sitting.

"So what are we supposed to do?" Jared asks, looking down at the paper Mr. Ikwang gave us.

I read it. "Case Study," it says. "A woman is arrested
for the kidnapping of her own child. The child, a two-
year-old girl, was last seen with the mother at the grocery

store on a Tuesday morning. On Wednesday, the girl was reported missing by the mother, who claimed an intruder came in during the night and took her."

"Wow," I say. "This is dark."

"Oh, look!" Lexi exclaims, her eyes sliding down the paper. "There are witnesses and everything! I want to play one of the witnesses!" She raises her eyes up and starts waving her hand in the air. "Mr. Ikwang, Mr. Ikwang, I want to play the part of 'witness number two, blond woman in the grocery store produce aisle,' please!'"

"Lexi!" Mr. Ikwang says. "I love your enthusiasm, but right now your group is supposed to be preparing some questions the prosecution might ask."

"This is like school," Lexi says glumly. She pushes the paper away.

"Yesterday's case was a lot more interesting," Luke says. He leans back in his chair, and I look over at him, still quite not believing he's my boyfriend. He's wearing a black sweater with a white T-shirt underneath and baggy jeans. Of course, the fact that he's hot is not why I like him. I like him because he's smart. Unlike Barelli, who apparently wishes he wasn't that smart and is very shallow.

"It was," Bailey says from the table behind us. She

flips her long curls over the shoulder of her tight pink sweater. "We couldn't stop debating it, it was driving us sooo crazy."

I'm not sure if she means "we" as in all of mock trial, or "we" as in her and Luke, but either way, I don't like it.

"Sounds fun," I say brightly, trying to pretend like everything's fine.

"So, are you guys going to the dance?" Bailey asks. She says 'you guys' but she's looking right at Luke. "Remember the last dance, Luke?" she says, before any of us can answer. "We didn't go because we decided to go four-wheeling at my uncle's instead."

"Yeah," Luke says, and he glances at me nervously. Probably because he knows he hasn't told me that he used to date her. Or about those notes they were passing, and who knows what else.

"It was sooo fun," Bailey goes on. Everything is "sooo" with her today. "Sooo" fun, "sooo" crazy. Ugh. Even though she's at another table, the back of her chair is close to Luke's, and she scoots it even closer toward him.

"Wasn't that where you had your first kiss?" Kim chimes in helpfully from next to her.

Lexi shoots her a death glare. "I'm not surprised

that you're so interested in who other people are kissing, Kim, since, you know, you like to figure it out and then just go after whoever it is."

Lexi's obviously talking about the Matt Connors situation that happened last month. Yikes. This could get heated. I glance nervously over at Mr. Ikwang, who's at the front of the room, talking animatedly to some kids about defendants' rights. Mr. Ikwang's pretty small. I don't know if he could break up Lexi and Kim if it came to that.

"Yeah, well, you know I'm *always* interested in that kind of stuff." And then Kim throws Jared a suggestive look. Lexi looks so mad I'm afraid she's going to fly across the table and maybe pull Kim's hair or something.

"I like to four-wheel, too," I blurt. Everyone looks at me in surprise. "Oh, yeah," I say. "I love four-wheeling. I used to always do it on my Grandpa Delaney's farm."

My Grandpa Delaney passed away when I was a baby, and I don't think he had a farm. But he totally could've. I don't really know much about him. So it's not exactly a lie, really.

"What kind of four-wheeler did you have?" Bailey asks. She's leaning over the back of her chair now, her long hair dangling down the side and her arm dangerously close to the back of Luke's shoulder.

"Umm . . . well . . ."

"You always used a Raptor this summer," Lexi chimes in helpfully. "You know, when you were visiting your grandma."

"Oh, right," I say, relieved. "That's a great four-wheeler." How does Lexi know about four-wheelers, anyway? She doesn't seem like that's her kind of thing.

"But I thought you weren't visiting your Grandpa Delaney this summer," Luke says, frowning. "You were visiting your other grandma, your mom's mom. Did you go four-wheeling there, too?"

And then something comes over me. Something very, very bad. The same sort of thing that came over me when I was away this summer. And before I know it, this is what I'm saying: "Well, actually, I didn't four-wheel at my grandma's *house.* I mean, I did it over the summer while I was visiting her. But the actual four-wheeling I did was at this guy Greg's house. My ex-boyfriend, Greg."

Ohmigod. Ohmigod. Ohmigod. What? Why? Why why why? Why did I just say that? I've now made up a guy named Greg who lives near my grandma, who I hung out with over the summer, and who took me four wheeling. None of which is true.

"Oh, right, Greg," Lexi says, not missing a beat, which is pretty impressive if you think about it. "He was so cute, he had that shaggy brown hair that you loved."

"I'm sure," Kim says, rolling her eyes.

"What's that supposed to mean?" Lexi demands.

"Nothing," Kim says, shrugging her delicate little shoulders. "Just that I'm sure he was cute."

"But that's not really how you said it," Lexi says. "Are you trying to imply that Devi can't get a cute guy?"

"Oh, please," Kim says. "Her name is Devon, not Devi."

"Are you calling Luke ugly?" Lexi asks. Jared, who's sitting next to her, looks a little nervous and puts his hand on Lexi's arm. "Because he's Devi's boyfriend. And if you think Devi can't get a hot guy, then what are you saying about Luke?"

"Any thoughts on the trial?" Mr. Ikwang asks, popping up from behind us. I almost scream, I'm so startled. But I'm also grateful that he saved me from what was becoming a very, very bad conversation.

"Uh, we're still looking it over," I tell him, giving him a big smile.

"I have a thought," Jared says.

"Yes, Jared?" Mr. Ikwang asks.

"Who's the father?" Jared leans forward and looks at Mr. Ikwang seriously.

Mr. Ikwang looks perplexed.

"The father of the baby," Jared explains. "Because usually the father is the one who steals the kids in these situations, isn't he?"

"The father passed away," Mr. Ikwang says, pointing to the case facts at the bottom of the sheet that tell us that.

"Yeah, but did he really?" Jared asks, looking pleased with himself. "Or are him and the mom kidnapping the baby, so that they can run away together?"

"Why would they have to kidnap their kid so they could run away together?" Lexi asks.

"Maybe he's married to someone else." Jared leans back in his chair and folds his arms over his chest. "I think this should be looked into."

"Very interesting, Jared," Mr. Ikwang says, even though he obviously thinks Jared is completely out of his mind. "And on that note, I think it's time to call it a day."

On the way out of mock trial, Barelli comes up to me and Luke and says, "Greg sounds really nice, Devon. I'd like to meet him sometime."

Then she smiles at me and passes by us out into the hall.

"That was nice of her," I say to Luke so that I don't seem like the jealous, overbearing girlfriend. What I don't say is that I'm sooo not falling for it.

chapter four

Luke and I sit on the bench outside of school and wait for our parents to pick us up. He reaches out and takes my hand, and a little thrill rushes through my body. I'm still not used to how it feels to actually be holding a boy's hand. I'm getting better, though. Like, I used to constantly worry about if my hand was sweaty or if I was holding his too hard. But now it feels more natural.

"So," Luke says.

"So," I say, swinging my legs underneath me.

"Listen, I need to ask you something," he says. "And it doesn't have to be weird, you know?"

"Oh?" My stomach does a flip. He's going to ask me to the dance! Finally! I put my best "don't worry of course I'm going to say yes" face on. It must be hard to be a guy, always having to worry about asking girls out, afraid of all that rejection. "Of course," I say seriously. "Go ahead."

He runs his fingers through his hair and then looks at me. "How come you didn't tell me you had a boy-friend this summer?"

Oh. Right. I take a deep breath and get ready to tell him that I didn't have a boyfriend this summer, that it was just something I kind of sort of made up, and that I'm so sorry but I wouldn't have had to do that if I knew what the deal was with him and Bailey and why won't he just ask me to the dance already?

"Luke, I—"

"Bye, Luke," Bailey calls as she bounces down the sidewalk in front of us. She took off the sweater she was wearing inside, and is now wearing a very tight, light blue V-neck with lace all around the collar. Gasp! She obviously just took her sweater off so that she could show off in front of Luke! I mean, come on! Why else would she take her sweater *off* before coming outside? It makes no sense.

"Bye," Luke says, giving her a wave.

"I don't know why I didn't tell you about my boyfriend," I say a little louder than is necessary, hoping that Barelli will overhear. But she doesn't seem to, and just goes flouncing away to the car that's waiting for her. In the driver's seat is someone who looks like an older version of Bailey. Probably her sister. Loud music is pumping from the car, and I can hear Bailey giggle at something her sister says as she hops in.

Just then, my dad's old Corolla pulls up next to us. Of course Bailey would be cool enough to have her sister picking her up, while I have to get picked up by my parents.

"There's your dad," Luke says, looking at the car. "You better go." He sounds annoyed.

"Are you mad at me?" I ask.

"I just don't understand why you wouldn't have told me about your old boyfriend."

"Well, you didn't tell me about Bailey," I say. "So I just figured we weren't going to have those kinds of conversations yet."

"Bailey?" Luke frowns, like he's never heard of her, and/or doesn't understand what she has to do with this conversation. Which is everything.

"Yeah, that you used to go out with her last year."

"I thought you knew about that," he says. "It's not like it was a secret."

"Well, I didn't," I say. I look to see if my dad's getting impatient, but he's on his cell phone. I can tell because his gesturing with his hands, and I can almost make out the Bluetooth in his ear. Probably on a business call.

"Oh, right," Luke says, pulling his hand away from mine. "That's because you liked Jared. You probably knew who *he* was dating."

"Not really," I mumble. I actually *did* know who Jared was dating, but that doesn't—wait a minute.

Is Luke jealous? Is that why he's acting so cranky all of a sudden? Is he jealous of this anonymous Greg person who doesn't even exist? Not that Luke *knows* he doesn't exist. In fact, as far as Luke knows, Greg could be some kind of totally hot guy, a four-wheeling champion who buys me flowers and kisses me. I feel a secret rush of excitement thinking about Luke being jealous of some other guy.

"Well, it would have been nice if you'd told me," he says.

"I'm sorry, I really am." I reach for his hand again, and give it a squeeze. "I should have told you, I just didn't think it was that big of a deal. Really, he meant nothing to me. He was nobody, just a . . . a summer fling!"

"Well then," Luke says. "If it was just a summer fling, I can see why you didn't mention it."

"Totally," I say, nodding. "He doesn't even cross my mind, not even a little." And then I remember Kim's doubtful comment in mock trial, and realize I need to make this sound as realistic as possible. "Of course," I add, "We still IM sometimes, but it's nothing, we're definitely just friends." People usually keep in touch with their ex-boyfriends, don't they? Bailey's still in touch with Luke. Of course, they do go to the same school, so it's a little different. But still.

Out of the corner of my eye, I can see my dad still on his phone call, but I stand up anyway. "I should go," I say. Luke stands up, and for a second, I wonder if he's going to kiss me in front of my dad.

"Well," he says. "I think I should meet him."

"My dad?" I ask. "Right now? Um, now's probably not the best time." The thing is, I kind of sort of haven't told my dad that Luke is actually my boyfriend. I mean, my parents know who Luke is and everything, but they don't know he and I are going out.

"Not your dad," Luke says, his blue eyes grim. "Greg."

"Oh," I say. "Right. Of course." Not. And then I wave goodbye and rush off to the car before he can realize I'm panicked.

When I get into the car, my dad quickly gets off his phone call. "Okay," he says briskly, "So we'll touch base about that on Monday." And then he gets a very guilty look on his face as he flips his phone shut and takes his Bluetooth out of his ear.

"Hi, honey," he says. "How was mock trial?"

"It was . . ." I grasp around in my head for something to say that won't exactly be a lie or sound too negative. "Interesting."

"You know, when I was in high school, I was in debate club."

"I know," I say as I buckle my seat belt. "One time mom showed me all your old debate club trophies." I hope he's not going to start telling me stories about debate club. Mock trial was boring enough.

"Well, I *was* the best in the state," he says, pulling the car onto the highway and looking pleased with himself. "I remember one time—" His cell phone starts ringing from his pocket, playing the tune of a rap song that I programmed on for him. If I can't have my own cell, then at least I should be able to have fun with someone else's, right?

"Aren't you going to answer that?" I ask, singing along with the song. It's very catchy. The song, I mean. And a very good temporary distraction from the fact that, you know, I've made up another fake boyfriend. Wow. That's my second fake boyfriend in six months. That has to be some kind of record.

"Uh, no," my dad says, "Probably nothing important."

"It could be very important," I say. "I know that if I had a cell phone, I would never, ever not answer it, since it could be you or mom calling me with some kind of family emergency." He raises his eyebrows. "And," I go on, "I could also use it to call you when I have to stay after school or something. Like today, when I had to use Lexi's phone to call you. I'm probably running up her bill super high. In fact, I should probably give her some money for that call I made today." This is pretty laughable, since Lexi's family has tons of money, and my dad knows it. But just because she has the money doesn't mean that I should take advantage of that, does it?

My dad's phone starts ringing again, and I reach over and grab it out of his shirt pocket before he can stop me.

"Devon, no!" he says, but I look at the screen before he can stop me.

"Calm down." I roll my eyes. "It's just Mom." I flip open his phone and answer it. "Hello?" I say.

"Hi, Devon," my mom says. "Listen, can you guys

stop at the store on the way home and pick up some milk?"

"Sure," I say. I can hear pots and pans clanging in the background, and then the phone gets muffled for a second and my mom says, "No, Katie, please don't pour ketchup into the stew!" And then the line goes dead.

"She wants us to pick up some milk," I say. I slide the phone shut and hold it out to my dad.

As I'm sliding it over, the phone starts ringing again. But my dad takes it out of my hand before I can see who it is, and shuts it off before putting it back in his pocket. Geez. Way to be the Phone Nazi.

The next morning at school, I head to Mel's locker first so that I can drop off our BFF notebook. The BFF notebook is something we started a while ago. We take turns writing notes back and forth in it, and then just pass the notebook to each other. It serves two purposes, in that we can pass it without teachers realizing that it's not school related, and we can keep our notes all in one place, so that we can read them back to each other one day when we're old and have grandchildren. Our plan is to talk about how much things have changed and how silly junior high was. Well, at least I'll hope that's what we'll do. It would be pretty upsetting if we read the notes and thought, "Oh, those were the days, when Devon made up fake boyfriends and Bailey Barelli was always around, like a little fly hovering, and oh, isn't it funny how Bailey married Luke?"

I slide the combination dial of Mel's locker to the left. Five . . . fifteen, twenty-one. Mel and I have each other's locker combinations just for situations like this. Wow, Mel really should clean this place once in a while. Her locker is pretty much a mess. Papers all over the place, which is really unlike her. Her bedroom is immaculate, you should see her bookshelves and her closet. Everything all facing the same way, color coded and alphabetized.

I move some papers out of the way so that I can put the notebook in, and as I do, some stuff falls onto the floor. Oopsies. I bend down to pick the papers up, and realize I've accidentally left a footprint on one of them. Hope it's not important. I look at the paper, "Application For . . ." is all I see before someone snaps it out of my hand.

"What are you doing?" Mel asks, slamming her locker door shut in front of me. She does it so fast that I almost lose my hand.

"I was just putting our notebook in your locker. You could have broken my fingers just now, you know?"

What is the deal with people being so secretive all of a sudden? First my dad and now Mel.

"Sorry," she mumbles. "It's just . . ." She shoves the paper she took from me into her bag.

"It's just what?"

"I dunno, I saw you looking at something, and I figured you might have been messing up something important." I look at her, and she slides her eyes down to the floor. Something's definitely going on here.

"Something's definitely going on here," I say.

"No, there isn't," she says.

"Yes, there is," I say.

"No."

"Yes."

"No."

"Then show me that paper!" I hold my hand out, waiting for her to hand it over.

"No!" she almost screams. "I mean, I can't. It's private."

"It's private?" I ask her incredulously. "Since when do we keep secrets?" Mel raises her eyebrows at me. Okay. So maybe I kind of sort of didn't tell Mel that my parents were having problems and were thinking about maybe getting divorced. And maybe Mel kind of sort of found out when her mom ran into my grandma at the store. But that was ages ago. Three weeks, at least.

"Okay," I say. "Point taken. But we've turned over a new leaf! I don't have any secrets from you right now. You know everything that's going on with me, and I want to know everything that's going on with you. We're BFF." Mel doesn't look convinced, so I rush on. "For example," I say. "Last night at mock trial I made up a fake boyfriend, and now Luke wants to meet him." I give her an encouraging smile. "Now you go."

"You what?!" Mel shrieks.

"Unh-uh," I say, wagging my finger at her. "Not until you tell me yours."

Mel takes a deep breath, "Devon, I—"

At that moment, a boy with blonde hair who's wearing a blue and white striped polo shirt passes by us in the hall. As he does, he gently tugs on Mel's hair. Then he turns around and winks at her. Mel blushes as red as a tomato.

"Who," I say, "was that?"

"Oh, that's Dylan," she says. She suddenly becomes very busy opening up her locker, turning the combination. But she's all flustered, and her hands slide past the numbers she needs.

"And who," I say, "is Dylan?" I've never heard of this Dylan, much less know why he'd be pulling Mel's hair. It seems very . . . flirty. Is this Mel's secret?

"He's just this guy who's in radio," she says. "We ended up talking for a little bit last night about broadcasting and stuff."

"Ooooh," I say, leaning against Mel's locker. "You guys were taaalking."

"Come on, Devon," she says, but her voice sounds like she's trying too hard to seem nonchalant. "He's an eighth grader."

"Ooooh," I say, "An eighth graaader."

Mel giggles and fake hits my shoulder. "Devon, come on, be serious."

"I am being serious. I mean, this sounds very serious." I look at her, and see her still blushing. "I thought you liked Brent Madison?"

Mel gives me a look, one of those "like that was ever going to happen" looks. I nod, but don't say anything. Besides him asking about her once when I ran into him at the mall, Mel hasn't had much success with Brent.

"So tell me about this Dylan," I say. I'm excited. New crush! Yay!

"Wellll." Mel finally has her locker open, and is collecting her books for her first class. "I don't really know that much, except like I said, he's in eighth grade. And very nice."

"Girlfriend?"

"I don't know. He didn't mention one." She looks nervous.

"Hmm. That could mean either he doesn't have one, or he just didn't want to mention her, which means he's a jerk." Mel's face falls at little at the thought of Dylan being a jerk. "But," I hurry on, "he just did some very public flirting with you, and why would he do that if he has a girlfriend?"

"I don't think he was flirting with me," Mel says, slamming her locker door shut. We fall into step together, heading down the hall, me toward English and her toward social studies.

"Um, he pulled your hair," I say. "That's most definitely flirting."

"It is?" We're at the door of my English class now, and we stop to talk for a second until the bell rings.

"Yes," I say. "It is. Now he's an eighth grader, so of course that means—"

"Who's an eighth grader?" Bailey Barelli asks, popping her head out of the classroom.

Great. Just how I want to start my morning! With Bailey Barelli asking me all sorts of annoying questions.

"No one," Mel says quickly, shooting me a look that lets me know she doesn't want anyone else knowing, even though it's totally unnecessary. Like I would ever tell Bailey Barelli anything about anyone.

"Yeah, no one," I say. I try to say it sort of short, so that Bailey knows I don't want to talk to her anymore. She's wearing this really fab red-and-white-striped top, and she has red clips in her hair holding back a little braid that goes to the side. It meets her curls and then falls all down her back. She looks like maybe she spent an hour getting ready this morning. I look down at my own outfit, a really cute white cotton dress with a pink butterfly on the bottom, over black leggings. Hmm.

"Ohhhh," Bailey says, in a very knowing tone. She smiles at me and Mel, like we're all friends. I guess she doesn't know she's the bane of my existence.

"What?" Mel asks.

"Yeah, what?" I ask, narrowing my eyes at her suspiciously.

"You must be talking about Greg, the guy you dated this summer. He's the one who's in eighth grade, right?"

"Who?" Mel asks. "I didn't date any guy named Greg this summer." I quickly step on her foot. "Ow!" she yells, "What'd you do that for?"

"Uh, sorry," I say. "Accident." And I do honestly

feel bad. Mel's wearing ballet flats, and I'm wearing chunky black shoes with a little bit of a heel. I must have really hurt her foot.

"Oh, how cute," Bailey says, but she doesn't sound like she thinks it's cute. "You didn't even tell Mel about Greg! Is that because he's an eighth grader?"

"Who's an eighth grader?" Luke says, coming up to us in the hall. Great.

"Greg is," Bailey says. She shrugs her shoulders. "Turns out Devi was dating an eighth grader over the summer, which is why no one really knew about it, even Mel. Is it because your parents wouldn't let you date older guys?"

Um, my parents won't let me date *any* guys. But I obviously can't say that. Because, you know, I'm dating Luke. And he's standing right there. "Um, not exactly," I say.

"You didn't tell me he was an eighth grader," Luke says.

"Well," Mel says. "It wasn't exactly that big of a deal, I mean, people date eighth graders all the time." I throw her a grateful smile, but Luke ignores her.

"An eighth grader!" he says again, sounding a little dazed.

"Luke, chill out," Bailey says. She reaches over

and squeezes his shoulder. "I mean, Devon said that we all could meet him, isn't that right, Devon?"

"No," I say, "I never said that."

Bailey blinks her eyes innocently. "I thought you mentioned something about us all getting together." "Us all"? Is Bailey Barelli crazy? How is it that she thinks there's an "us all"? It sounds suspiciously like she thinks there's going to be some sort of double date, her and Luke, and me and this Greg person.

"Well," I say slowly. "I'm not sure how that would work exactly, since, you know, he lives so far away."

Bailey waves her hand like this is nothing. "Not a big deal," she says. "I once dated a guy who lived in a whole other state. We met at summer camp. Besides, my mom is always around and she loves to drive and pick people up."

"Well, great," I say. "Maybe sometime we can all meet up." A summer camp boyfriend? How many ex-boyfriends has Barelli had? I can hardly keep up with my one. Of course, mine is fake, and hers are probably real. But still.

"Actually, I'm having a party," Bailey says, smiling all innocently up from under her long lashes. She definitely has mascara on. "It's my birthday."

"That's right," Luke says, smiling.

What? Why? How is it he can remember his ex-girlfriend's birthday, and not remember that there is a very big semiformal coming up to which I am currently dateless?

"Anyway, you should all come," Bailey says. "It's on Saturday." She's having a boy/girl party? Great. I've never been to a boy/girl party. But of course I can't tell her that. She's probably been having tons of boy/girl parties since she was five. Not to mention all the boy/girl parties she's probably *been* to. And I know Luke's been to boy/girl parties, since he's always been A-list, and they have tons of those things.

"Sure," I say. "I'll come." No way I'm letting Luke go by himself to Bailey Barelli's birthday party. Hmm. I wonder if he'll get her a present. Do I have to get her a present? Probably, otherwise she'd know that I didn't get her one just because I don't like her. I wonder if Luke and I can get her a joint present. Something kind of generic, like a scented candle or a journal. Perfectly nice, but not that personal. And I'll sign the card, "Best, Devon and Luke." Definitely not 'love.'

"Great!" Bailey says. "And make sure you bring Greg."

"I'll ask him," I say. "But I'm not sure he can make it."

Kim Cavalli comes up to us at that moment, which makes no sense, because I know for a fact that her first class is math, which is on the complete other side of the school, and the bell is about to ring in one second. I guess she doesn't care about being late. She's wearing super big hoop earrings that almost touch her neck, and her hair is in a ponytail.

"Ohmigod," she says. "What's going on out here?" But she smiles when she says it, like she can't imagine anything could possibly be going on, since she's not involved.

"I was just inviting everyone to my party," Bailey says. "Devon's going to bring Greg."

"Well," I say. "I said I'd ask him if he wants to go."

"It seems like maybe you don't want to bring him," Luke says. He looks slightly upset.

"It's not that I don't want to," I say. starting to feel a little sick to my stomach. Why isn't the bell ringing? Seriously, every time you want or need the bell to ring, it never does. "I just can't promise that he's going to come."

"He might be sick." Mel, who up until this point has been pretty quiet, offers up this gem.

"Sick?" Kim laughs. Her earrings sparkle, catching the light as she moves. "Why, what's wrong with him?"

"Nothing's wrong with him," Mel says. "He just sometimes . . ." She trails off.

"Gets sick," I finish for her, lamely. "He has a very compromised immune system."

"Eww," Bailey says. "That sounds gross." She wrinkles her tiny little nose and pushes her hair out of her face. Ohmigod. Is Barelli wearing a nose ring? She is! A little nose jewel right on the side of her nose. It's one of those stick-on ones, obviously, since she didn't have it yesterday.

"It's not gross," I say, not wanting Luke to think that the guy I dated before him was gross. "I had to take care of him a lot."

"Because of his compromised immune system?" Kim looks at me skeptically. "Well, hopefully he can make it on Saturday. I mean, after that whole thing with you making up a fake relationship with Jared, it would be nice if you could prove you were trustworthy."

I'm about to ask her to whom, exactly, I have to prove I'm trustworthy. Her? Barelli? The only people in this group I owe anything to are Luke and Mel. And Mel already knows the truth. And Luke, well . . . I sigh.

"Don't worry," I say. "He'll be there."

chapter five

"Are you crazy?" Lexi asks me. We're in Callie's Closet, a consignment store a few blocks from my school that always has name brand stuff super cheap. We walked here after the last bell rang, which of course, constituted me using Lexi's cell again. Totally ridiculous. "Why would you tell her *Greg* is going to come?"

"I don't know," I moan, flipping my way through a rack of skinny jeans. "It was Kim! She brought up the whole lying-about-Jared thing, and before I knew it, it just happened." I lower my voice to a horrified whisper. "I cracked under the peer pressure."

"Ugh, Kim," Lexi says, shaking her head. "That girl is lethal." She comes over to the rack I'm at and holds up a turquoise sweater. "Cute or ugly?"

"Cute," I tell her. I hold up a pair of jeans and eye the price tag. Hmm. "Is it worth paying this much for something that's probably just a fad?"

"How many times do I have to tell you," Lexi says. "Skinny jeans are not a fad."

"Anything that's only going to last a season or two is definitely a fad." I add them to the pile of stuff in my arms anyway.

"Ooh," Lexi says, looking at a Versace dress that's hanging on the wall. "That is absolutely fabulous." She rushes over and checks the price tag. "You should try it on." Lexi likes shopping here because she can find staples, like sweaters and jeans, and maybe some shoes. But Lexi can afford to buy the current season's name brand stuff, so she doesn't really *need* to shop here.

"Luke hasn't even asked me to the dance yet," I say. "So I don't have to worry about finding a dress." And even if I did have to worry about it, I couldn't afford that dress. Even at consignment shop prices. I sigh and put the pile of stuff I'm holding down on a rack. I probably shouldn't be buying anything. I need to save my allowance for a dress just in case.

"He's totally going to ask you!" Lexi snaps her gum. "Ooh, vintage!" She holds up a pair of Prada shoes that can't be more than two seasons old. She puts one on her foot and then frowns. "Hmm, do these make me look like I have cankles?"

"Lexi!" I say. "Please focus!" Lexi does not have cankles. "Some of us have real problems, like a fake ex-boyfriend, ever heard of it?"

"Well, you already got out of one fake ex-boyfriend mess, how much worse can another one be?"

"You did not just ask me that," I say. I pick up a bracelet off of a jewelry tray and hold it up to my wrist.

"Devon," Lexi says. "I don't want to hear this negative attitude that is now permeating the store."

"Did you just say 'permeating'?"

"Totally," Lexi says. "It's one of our English vocab words." She smiles. Lexi has new braces. Light blue. Very cute. She also has a real boyfriend that asked her to the dance. I try not to feel jealous.

"This is not the end of the world." It sure feels like it. I follow Lexi obediently to the register. "Aren't you getting anything?" she asks.

"Not today. I don't have any money, and the money I do have, I'm saving for the dress just in case Luke does ask me." I'm enjoying feeling very sorry for myself as Lexi checks out. She spends over four hundred dollars on jeans, shoes, and accessories, all on a prepaid credit card that her mom gave her. *My* mom is supposed to be picking us up, so we head outside to wait.

A few raindrops are falling from the sky, and there's no sign of my mom, so Lexi and I decide to head into the coffee shop next door. We order cappuccinos with extra vanilla shots and sit down in some squashy chairs by the window.

"Hmm," Lexi says, once we're settled in. "I have a fab idea! Let's make a list!"

"A list of what?" I ask warily. Last time Lexi wanted to make a list, we ended up listing all the clothes she owned, plus possible outfit combinations. *So* not the way I want to spend my afternoon.

"Ways to get out of the whole Greg situation!" She reaches into her bag, rummages around, and pulls out a purple notebook with a big swirly "A" embossed in gold on the bottom, for her full name: Alexis.

I take a sip of my cappuccino, letting the warmth of the foam slide down my throat. I check my watch. My mom is twenty minutes late now, but I don't even care. Once we get into my mom's car, there's no way we'd be able to talk about this.

"Now," Lexi says, tapping her pen against the paper and looking thoughtful. "We need to come up with options."

"Options," I repeat.

"Yeah," she says. "Of things we can do to fix this whole problem."

"Um, move far away and/or transfer to boarding school?" I try.

Lexi nods seriously and writes "Move away and/or go to boarding school" on her pad.

"I was joking," I say.

"Oh." Lexi crosses out what she just wrote, and then, thinking better of it, pulls the top sheet off her pad and crumples it up into a ball.

"It's hopeless," I tell her, dropping my head onto the table. "Just hopeless." What is wrong with me? Have I not learned my lesson? Maybe I should just tell everyone the truth. Luke will break up with me, Kim and Bailey will laugh behind my back, but at least my life will be less complicated. A nice, completely normal, uncomplicated life. That sounds very nice.

"Hey," Lexi says, looking over my shoulder. "Isn't that your dad?"

I turn around and see my dad coming into the coffee shop. "Finally," I say, standing up. My mom must have gotten tied up doing something for work, and sent my dad to get me instead.

"Dad," I start to call, but then I stop. Because behind him is a tall blond woman wearing a business suit and carrying a briefcase. A tall blond woman who follows my dad up to the counter and orders a latte. A tall blond woman who then sits with my dad at a table. A tall blond woman who makes Lexi go, "uh-oh," under her breath. A tall blond woman who is definitely not my mother.

"Devon, you can't jump to conclusions," Mel says. It's later that night, and I'm sitting on her bed, cross-legged. Lexi's there too, on the floor, flipping through a magazine.

"Mel, he was at a coffee shop with another woman," I tell her. I lean over the bed and pull the hair tie out of my hair, letting it brush against the floor, all the blood rushing to my head.

After Lexi and I spotted my dad with the mystery woman, we tried to get close to where they were sitting, and I swear I overheard my dad say "when we move." Hello! He's planning on moving in with this woman! Will I have to go too? Will I have to switch schools? What will my mom do? Where will Katie live?

Lexi and I laid low, and finally, they left. About five minutes later my mom pulled up in front of the coffee shop. Apparently, she thought my dad was supposed to pick me up, which was why she was late. I didn't have the heart to tell her what I saw.

"Maybe he meant 'when we move tables' or something," Mel offers.

"Maybe," I say, flipping myself back over. I look over at Lexi. "Did it seem like that's what he meant?"

"No," she says, still paging through the magazine.

"Ugh," I say. My head feels all wobbly. I can't tell if it's because of my dad or because I was hanging upside down.

"This isn't that big of a deal." Lexi shrugs. "I mean, affairs happen. It's totes the hip thing these days."

"Totes?" Mel asks, confused.

"It means 'totally,'" I explain. "Anyway, I don't care if it's the new hip thing, my dad might be cheating on my mom!"

"And would that *really* be the end of the world?" Lexi asks. She takes a sip from her diet Coke. "Remember this summer when your parents were having problems and they felt so guilty about it that they sent you away to be with your grandma?"

"Yes!" I say. "It was awful."

"But you had all those cute clothes," Lexi points out. I stare at her blankly. Is she really saying that it will be okay if my parents are having problems because at least I will have cute clothes? She flips another page in the magazine. "Ooh," she says, holding it up to show us, "I told you skinny jeans aren't just a fad!" Apparently she is.

"My life is a mess," I say. I tick the reasons off on my fingers. "One, my parents are maybe possibly getting divorced. Two, Luke has not asked me to the dance. Three, Bailey Barelli is demanding I bring my fake boyfriend to her stupid, dumb boy/girl party that I don't even want to go to." A piece of my Passion Plum nail polish flakes off and lands on my fingertip. "And now my manicure is ruined."

"Here," Lexi says, pulling a free sample of perfume out of the magazine she's reading. "You can have the free sample." She generously sets it down on the bed next to me.

"Thanks," I say. I open it up, and a flowery scent fills the room. I rub some on my wrists and all over my neck, but it doesn't make me feel better. How did everything become so complicated? I thought my parents were getting back on track. They were seeing Dr. Meyerson, they were working on their harsh tones . . .

why would my dad *do* something like this?

"Hey," Mel says, sitting down on the bed next to me. "I'm sure that it's nothing."

"You are?" I search her face for any kind of insincerity, any clue that she's just saying this to make me feel better.

"Definitely," she says. "That woman was probably just someone from your dad's work."

"You think?"

"Totally," Mel says. "You just need to talk to him about it, and then you'll feel better."

"Now let's work on your fake boyfriend issue!" Lexi says excitedly. I sigh. That seems pretty unimportant now in the grand scheme of things.

"The fake boyfriend issue," Mel says. "Is actually pretty easy to fix."

"It is?" I ask, interested in spite of myself.

"Yes," Mel says. "Because you're both missing something here."

"The fact that Devi should have learned her lesson about fake boyfriends?" Lexi asks.

"No," Mel says.

"The fact that I should be secure in my womanhood and my relationship and just be able to ask Luke what is going on?" I try.

"No," Mel says.

"Those are both very good points," I say. Lexi nods.

"Those *are* very good points," Mel says. "But what's done is done." She takes the empty perfume sample out of my hands and drops it into the garbage. "Devon, what does your new fake boyfriend have that your old fake boyfriend doesn't?"

I think hard. "I dunno," I say. I haven't really created him yet. I try to think of something that my new fake boyfriend would have. Something that Jared, my old fake boyfriend, doesn't. Something that would make Luke very, very, jealous. Millions of dollars? No, Luke's not that materialistic. Maybe he's a prince? Nah, then I'd have to move to a foreign country, and since Luke is so into mock trial, I'm guessing he's pretty patriotic. "His own four-wheeler?" I try.

"Ooh!" Lexi says. She raises her hand like we're at school and looks proud of herself. "He wants to be Devon's date for the dance!"

Mel looks at us like we're crazy and/or stupid. "No," she says. "He's *fake.*" She sits back on the bed and crosses her arms like she's proud of herself.

"But Jared was fake, too," I remind her. "Hence the term 'fake boyfriend.'"

"Nooo," Mel says, rolling her eyes at me. "Jared

was real, he just wasn't your boyfriend. Greg is fake."

"So how does that help her?" Lexi asks.

"No one knows who he is," Mel says. "He could be anybody." Her brown eyes sparkle with mischief. And then it dawns on me. Mel is right. No one knows this alleged Greg. He could be anyone.

"I don't get it," Lexi says.

"She means that all we have to do, is find someone to be Greg!" I stare at Mel in awe. "Mel, you're a genius!"

"You mean we're going to hire an actor?" Lexi looks excited. "I've always wanted to be a casting director."

"I don't think we can hire an actor," I say, "I mean, we don't have any money." Well, Lexi does. But I don't think it would be fair to ask her to finance a fake ex-boyfriend. "So who do we know?" I run through a list of people in my head, hot guys that I know who have never met any of my school friends.

"What about Jack?" Mel asks. "He's always had a little bit of a thing for you."

"He has?" I didn't know that. Jack is Mel's cousin, and I never knew he had a thing for me. How much of a thing, I wonder? Not that I would ever want to date him. Jack is kind of . . . bizarre. He's into role-playing games, like dressing up like a wizard and/or acting out Harry Potter scenes. I've only met him a couple times, but I don't think he's what I had in mind when I pictured Greg. Still, maybe beggars can't be choosers.

"Is he hot?" Lexi asks.

"Ummm . . ." I look at Mel, not sure what to say. How do I diss her cousin without sounding like a total brat? Plus, I should be nice to him. I mean, he's obviously in love with me. And what if he somehow found out what I said about him? I don't want to crush the poor boy's heart. He's probably very—

"He has a girlfriend," Mel says.

"Girlfriend? I thought he liked *me.*" Figures.

"Well, he's not pining over you or anything; he's only met you a couple of times."

"Yes, but is he hot?" Lexi asks.

Mel and I don't say anything.

"You need someone hot," Lexi goes on. She pulls her cell phone out of her bag and slides her finger down her list of contacts. "Let's see, who do I know? Josh? No, he sometimes starts sweating when he gets nervous." She bites her lip. "Yes!" she exclaims finally. "Ryan Geist! He's perfect!"

"He is?"

"Yes, and he's totally hot and cool." She slides her phone back into her bag. "I'll call him tonight and ask if he can play your boyfriend at the party."

I stand up and clap my hands. "Yay!"

"Isn't it going to be a little hard for him to pretend he knows Devon?" Mel asks.

"No, we'll train him." Lexi says. She smiles. "Easy peasy. Now we just need to figure out what we're going to wear. You guys want to go shopping tomorrow?"

"We just went shopping today," I point out.

"You can never go shopping too much," Lexi says. "Besides, we need to get new outfits. I mean, there's probably going to be spin the bottle." She looks at Mel. "You should invite Dylan." Mel looks a little sick at this possibility.

There's a knock on her bedroom door, and Mel's mom appears. She's wearing her work clothes, a sleek black suit with pinstripes. Very smart and professional looking.

"Hi, girls," her mom says. "Are you two going to be staying for dinner?"

"Uh, no," Mel says quickly. I frown. What does she mean, "no"? I'd like to stay for dinner. Working out the fake boyfriend issue was a nice distraction, but now I'm back to thinking about my parents. And I don't think I can face my dad right now. Or my mom. I mean, what would I say? Should I tell my mom what I saw? Should

I confront my dad? I feel the backs of my eyes start to get all prickly, and I take a deep breath to try and keep myself from crying.

"Are you sure they can't stay?" Mel's mom asks. "I'm making lasagna."

"No," Mel says forcefully. And then she gives her mom a look. A look that is suspiciously like the one I gave Mel this morning in the hallway, when I was trying to convey something to her without anyone else noticing. Which means that Mel is trying to tell her mom something that she doesn't want me and Lexi to know. And it has to do with why she doesn't want us staying for dinner.

"I actually can't stay," I say, so Mel won't feel uncomfortable. "My mom's making her famous four-alarm chili, and she'd kill me if I wasn't there." A total lie. But honestly, what's one more?

Besides, that's the least of my worries. The most being, you know, my dad; the second being, Luke not asking me to the dance. And now I have to add to the list whatever Mel is hiding from me.

When I get home, no one's in the kitchen, even though it's dinnertime. I find Katie sitting in the living room, in front of the TV. She's watching MSNBC.

"Where're Mom and Dad?" I kick off my shoes and plop down onto the couch.

"Upstairs," she says. "They are having a talk, and asked to not be disturbed, please."

Uh-oh. That doesn't sound good. A talk? That they don't want to be disturbed from? Nothing good ever comes from talks that people don't want to be disturbed from.

"Did they say what it was about?" I ask nonchalantly. I pull my assignment book down and scroll down my list. Ugh. I have a chapter to read for history, plus a bunch of English homework. Could this day get any worse?

"No," Katie says. "It's for grown-ups *only*." She looks at me with disdain, like I obviously do not understand things that are for grown-ups.

"Can you turn that down?" I ask. It's time to eavesdrop, and on the TV, two newscasters are arguing about something, which is going to make listening in on my parents' conversation almost impossible. "Why are you watching this anyway?"

"It is about current events." She holds the remote close to her, like she's afraid I'm going to take it away from her. Which I was considering. "'Current' means things that are happening now."

"I know what 'current' means," I tell her. "But why are you watching it? Isn't there a *Blue's Clues* episode on somewhere that you should be tuning into?"

"I don't watch *Blue's Clues*!" Katie's distressed. "*Blue's Clues* is for babies!"

"Well, excuuuse me," I say. "I don't keep up with what kindergarteners are watching these days." I know this will make her happy, since she's only in preschool. She loves when anyone thinks she's in kindergarten. And then I see the graphics and text on the screen under the faces of the newscasters. "International committee looks into alleged Olympic rowing scandal." Well, that explains it. Katie's feeding her Olympic obsession.

"Well," I say, making a big show of standing up and stretching. "I guess I'm just going to go upstairs and start on all this homework." I give my bag a pat and even add in a fake yawn for good measure. What I'm really going to do is spy on my parents. But as I'm standing up, it becomes unnecessary, since their voices come tumbling down the stairs. They're not yelling exactly, but their voices are definitely raised.

"I was late, John. It happens," my mom says. My dad must be upset with her for picking me up late. Is it possible that maybe he saw me at the coffee shop?

89

Otherwise, why would he be so upset? "I don't understand what the big deal is."

"The big deal is that . . ." the rest of what my dad says is too muffled to understand.

Katie looks at me, her eyes wide. "Harsh tones," she whispers. She pushes her bangs out of her face.

"Hey," I say, "Don't worry about it." I get down on the floor and wrap my arms around her. "It's just some harsh tones, big deal." I roll my eyes. "I mean, come on. Asking someone to never have harsh tones? That's just silly."

"But that's what they're supposed to be doing. No. Harsh. Tones!"

"They're not going to be perfect," I say. "They're working on it, and everything's fine."

Katie smiles at me and then turns her attention back to the Olympic rowing scandal. Wow. Talk about bouncing back. Too bad I don't believe what I just told her. It's more than obvious that my dad is very upset about me being at the coffee shop, and it's probably because he realizes just how close he came to being caught. And my poor mom has no idea why he's so upset about everything, and she just thinks he's taking all these harsh tones with her for no reason. And no matter what I tell Katie, there is nothing good about this situation. Not one single thing. Not—

My mom comes clomping down the stairs. "Devon," she announces. "You're getting a cell phone."

Well. I guess there's that.

"I'm getting a cell phone after school today," I tell Luke the next morning at school. He's waiting for me at my locker, looking extremely cute in a pair of khaki pants and a blue T-shirt.

"That's awesome," Luke says. "Now we can text all during school."

"Yeah," I say, turning away before he can see that I'm blushing. He wants to text with me all during school! I mean, come on! He wouldn't want to text with me all day if he still liked Barelli. He wouldn't want to be in *constant contact* with me if I wasn't his one and only. As if on cue, Luke's phone beeps, and he pulls it out of his pocket, checks the screen, and then starts typing on his keyboard. Hmm. Well, of course he's going to be texting with other people. I mean, everyone does it. Everyone who has a cell phone. And now I will too! Who is he texting with, though, I wonder? Jared maybe? But then I see Jared down the hall, standing with Lexi. His phone is nowhere to be seen. So not Jared. Maybe a friend from soccer? Maybe his mom? I try to look over and check his screen, but I can't see anything without leaning in too much, which would be totally obvious.

"Are you looking at my phone?" Luke asks.

"No," I say. "I mean, well, yeah, but only because I wanted to see if I should get the same kind as you."

"You should get whatever one you like," Luke says. And then all of a sudden, his voice turns serious. "Listen, Devon," he says, and slides his phone into his pocket. He leans against the locker next to mine. Ohmigod. He's going to tell me he was texting Bailey. And yeah, he's probably going to say they're just friends, but who really believes that? And if they're texting all day, then why do they have to note-pass on top of it?

I put on my best "I'm totally adjusted and don't care about any of this" face.

"I need to, uh, to ask you something."

"Yes, Luke?"

He looks down at the floor, and mumbles something that sounds like, "Wilahslhdwishme."

"What?" I ask.

"Will you go to the dance with me?" He looks up at me, and his blue eyes meet mine, and I'm so shocked that at first I'm sure I couldn't have heard him right. But then Mikayla Parsons, this very loud eighth grader, who always wears a bomber jacket to school, steps on my foot as she walks by me in the hall, and I realize Mikayla Parsons stepping on my foot would never happen if this were just a dream.

"Of course!" I say. Which, you know, may be a little eager, but days of anticipation and waiting will do that to a person.

Luke smiles and leans over and brushes his lips against mine. My stomach goes all wobbly and I lean back against my locker and try to catch my breath.

"Hey," Lexi says, walking up to us in the hall. "You two are sooo cute, but seriously, can we keep the PDA for after school?" But she's smiling.

"Ha-ha," I say, rolling my eyes, even though it makes me happy that she noticed. I have a boyfriend who wants to kiss me in the halls at school! A very cute, very smart, very amazing boyfriend who wants to kiss me, me, me. And not Barelli.

I can't believe I was ever worried about him asking me to the dance! I mean, hello. He's like obviously totally in love with me. And Bailey and her long hair and alabaster skin can do nothing to sway him! Actually I think alabaster skin means pale or something. And Bailey is always quite tan. No matter! I'm going to the dance with Luke! Yay!

"Luke and I were just talking about the dance," I say, giving Lexi a look.

"Ooh!" she says, "So he finally—uh, so you guys are going?"

"Yeah," Luke says.

"You'll have to ride over with me and Jared." Lexi claps her hands. "And we'll have an after party at my house, of course, and maybe even a pre-party." She frowns. "Of course, I'll have to think up a theme." She looks off into space thoughtfully. A theme? Hmm. I hope she doesn't expect me to dress up for the theme or anything. I need a dress for the dance, not for Lexi's pre-parties and after parties and all her in-between parties. Plus, I'm going to have a hard enough time convincing my parents that I'm allowed to go to the dance at all, much less all these other parties. I haven't even told them about Bailey's party yet.

"Hey, guys," Kim says as she slides down the hall. "Luke, Lexi." She looks at me. *"Devi."* Kim likes to call me Devi with this little snort at the end, like it's not quite my name. She thinks it's super funny to mock it.

"Oh, hi, Kim," Lexi says. "Love your top. I think it's great that someone with such skinny legs isn't afraid to go for vertical stripes." She smiles, and Kim gives her a thin smile back.

"Thanks," she says. "I actually got it the other night when I was shopping for something new to wear to Bailey's party." She looks me up and down. "You guys are still going, right?"

"Yes," Luke says, a little too fast for my liking. Why's he so anxious to get to Bailey's party? I wonder if he bought her a present yet. Hopefully something generic, like a gift card. Or a gag gift, like the time my dad got an ant farm from my Uncle Thomas.

"Of course you're going to be there, Luke," Kim says. "Bailey told me how well you used to get along with her family." Luke gets a little half smile on his face, like he's remembering Bailey's family fondly. Figures. My family doesn't even know he exists. Well, they do. Just not as my boyfriend.

"We're definitely going to be there," Lexi says. "We're so excited, we wouldn't miss it for the world. And my mom's going to pick up Greg, so you'll get to meet him."

A flicker of uncertainty passes over Kim's face for a second, but she recovers quickly. I shoot Lexi a look, but she just smiles and says, "Right, Devi?"

"Right." She must have talked to her friend Ryan! Yay! Now all I have to do is get through this dumb party, show off Ryan/Greg for a couple of hours, and everything will be fine.

chapter six

My mom picks me up after mock trial that day, so that we can go shopping for my new cell phone. My idea, not hers. I figured if my parents were having some kind of weird meltdown where they thought me getting a cell phone was okay, then I needed to capitalize on it before they changed their minds. So I insisted we go ASAP.

"How was mock trial?" she asks, as I vault myself into the minivan.

"It was good," I lie. Mock trial was definitely not good. Lexi skipped so she could go and hang out with Jared, and I had to be in a group with Kim, Bailey,

Luke, and Kim's on-again, off-again boyfriend, Matt Connors. The whole thing was extremely annoying, since Bailey kept touching Luke's arm every single time she thought he said something funny. And then when my mom pulled up, I had to leave them in the lobby, ALONE. TOGETHER. And Luke couldn't even walk me out or hold my hand or kiss me goodbye, because, hello, what if my mom saw?

To add insult to injury, all during science today Mel planned out her radio show, which is going to be an advice and gossip show! Where people call in and ask her advice! Hello! Advice and gossip is totally up my alley. I mean, I'm a master at getting out of tricky situations. Her class advisor said she could find a partner to do it with her, but I just don't have the time with mock trial.

"Where are we going?" Katie asks as my mom pulls out of the school.

"Oh," I say, looking into the backseat. "I didn't know you were here."

"I'm here!" Katie says, giving me a big grin.

"Great," I say. Katie tends to throw tantrums in stores. She starts out strong, but then gets very cranky the longer we end up staying there. If she does something to ruin my chance of finally getting a cell, I'm going to be very mad.

"So, anyway," I say to my mom. "I wanted to ask you about a couple of things."

"Okay," my mom says. She looks pretty today. She's wearing a rose colored, button up sweater over a white T-shirt, and it brings out her eyes.

"Well," I say, "Lexi and Mel are going to this dance next weekend, and I was wondering if I could go, too." None of this is a lie. Lexi *is* going to the dance, and I'm pretty sure Mel will be going, too, even if she just comes along with us. And I didn't *exactly* say I would be going *with* them, although of course I will be. There will just be some boys there as well. But my mom doesn't need to know every single person that I'm going to be hanging out with, does she? She lets me go lots of places where she doesn't know every single person that's going to be there. Like school, for example.

"Sure," my mom says. "Do you need a dress?"

Wow. That was easy. "Yes," I tell her. "Not too fancy . . . but not too unfancy, either. It's a semi-formal."

Katie leans her head through the space between the front seats. "Fancy, fancy, fancyyy," she sings.

"What's that on your head?" I ask.

"Swimming cap. I'm going to be an Olympic swimmer."

"Oh, how fun," I tell her. I reach into my bag, pull out a piece of gum, and pop it into my mouth. "Too bad you're scared of the water."

"No, I'm not!"

"Yes, you are."

"No, I'm not!"

"Yes, you are. Remember when you signed up for swimming lessons and you couldn't even stick your face in the water or take off your water wings?"

"Devon," she tells me seriously. "All Olympic athletes have to work hard to achieve their goals."

"Katherine Delaney," my mom says. "Sit back in your seat right now."

Katie obeys.

"So anyway," I say. "Not too fancy, but something a little fancy." Maybe with sparkles. Or a long, flowing train. Hmm. In lavender. Or pink. Pastels, definitely.

"Okay," my mom says, turning the minivan onto the highway. "This weekend we'll head down to Morty's."

"Oh, um, well, actually, I was hoping I could go shopping with Lexi for my dress." Morty's is a department store in the mall, which isn't necessarily *bad*, it's just not what I'm looking for.

"You don't want to go shopping with me?" My mom looks hurt.

"No, I do," I say, deciding it's time to change the subject. "But that was the other thing I was going to ask you about. This weekend my, uh, friend Bailey Barelli is going to be having some people over, so I was wondering if I could go over, too. We'll probably work on mock trial."

"But you hate Bailey Barelli," Katie says from the backseat. She's moving all around back there, and her knees keep kicking the back of my seat.

"No, I don't," I say, shooting Katie a look. "We're in mock trial together," I explain to my mom, as if that makes us BFF.

"No, you think she's going to steal your *boy*friennnd." Katie sings the word 'boyfriend' like she's Avril Lavigne.

"Yeah, right," I say, hoping I sound light and airy. "If I even *had* a boyfriend."

"Yes, you do have a *boy*friennnd," Katie says. "Luke and Devon, sittin' in a tree, K-I-S-S-I-N-G. First comes love, then comes marriage, then comes Devon with a baby carriage!" Katie collapses into giggles, but my mom doesn't think it's so funny. She has a stricken look on her face as she pulls off at our exit.

"Devon, is that true?"

"No!" I say, but she raises her eyebrows. Outside,

the houses on the street go flying by, and suddenly, I feel hot. I reach over and turn down the stream of warm air my mom has pumping into the car, and crack my window just a little bit.

"He kissed her," Katie reports. "I saw them one time." She wrinkles her nose. "It was *very* gross."

"Devon, I've told you it's perfectly fine for you to have an interest in boys," my mom says. "And I would hope that if Luke was your boyfriend, you wouldn't lie about it."

"Okay," I say, "but he's not my boyfriend."

"Good, because you are much too young to have a boyfriend!" my mom exclaims.

"But you just said that I could tell you if I had one, and that I shouldn't hide it from you!" Hmmm. Is my mom getting senile? She pulls into the parking lot of the cell phone store. I really hope this whole having a boyfriend thing doesn't put her off getting me a phone. Seriously, could Katie's timing be any worse? And when did she see us kiss, anyhow? Luke only kisses me sometimes, like when we're saying goodbye to each other.

"When did you see us kiss?" I whisper to Katie as we're getting out of the car.

"When Luke came over that one night, when you were supposed to be babysitting me," Katie says. She's talking about a night a couple of weeks ago, when Luke showed up at our house unannounced when my parents weren't home. I got caught, of course, and got into tons of trouble. But that was way before Luke was even my boyfriend. And so we were certainly not kissing.

"We didn't kiss that night," I say, slamming the car door.

Katie shrugs and jumps down from the back of the van. Whatever.

I link one arm through my mom's, one arm through Katie's, and start marching us toward the doors. "Now, time to get me a phone!"

"I didn't say it was okay for you to have a boyfriend," my mom's saying as I pull her along.

"You didn't?" I ask warily.

"I said if you *did,* you shouldn't lie about it." She sighs and takes Katie's hand as we walk into the store. "We'll discuss this later." I hope she means much later. As in never. And especially not with my dad around.

Once we're in the store, Katie heads for the phones that are on display, and picks up a black flip phone. She pushes the buttons and says, "Hello, White House? This is Katie Delaney, calling you about the Olympic rowing scandal."

I head toward the front of the store, where there's

a big sign that says JUST IN in light blue writing. On the table is a display of phones that have little keyboards and covers that slide up. They come in all different colors—red, orange, yellow, blue. I pick up the purple one and show it to my mom. "It's this one!" I announce. "This is the one that I want!"

My mom looks it over. "I don't know, Devon," she says. "This one looks a little flashy."

"It's very teen friendly," the clerk says, appearing from nowhere. His nametag says, "Jeffrey" and he has earrings all up his ear. How cool.

"Perfect!" I say. I pick it up and look at it again. So cute! And with the slide out keyboard, I'll be a texting machine. I run my hands over it and practice a little bit.

"It's perfect for texting," Jeffrey says.

"Thanks, Jeffrey," I say. "That's very helpful."

From behind me, I can hear Katie saying, "I'd like to speak with the head of the Olympic committee, please," into the phone she's holding.

"I don't think you really need to be *texting*," my mom says, like it's a bad word or something.

"Oh, everyone texts these days," Jeffrey says, waving his hand as if he's brushing her comment off. He sounds cheerful. "Even my grandmother texts."

"Come on, Mom," I say, "It's not like I'm going

to be texting in school or anything." Well, not during class at least.

She bites her lip. "I just don't know if I like what's happening here. First you have some kind of secret boyfriend, and now you're getting a phone to text." I want to tell her that at least my secret boyfriend is real and I just haven't mentioned him, not like my former fake boyfriend and my current fake ex-boyfriend. Wow. I'm really confusing myself.

"I don't have a boyfriend," I say. "Secret, rumored, or otherwise." Lie, lie, lie.

Jeffrey looks from my mom to me and back. "So should I ring this up or . . . ?"

"Yes," I say, handing it to him. We both follow him to the register, navigating our way through the shiny cases of cell phones. This store is very cool. I might even like it better than the mall.

"What about that one?" My mom points to a phone that's sitting in the front case. It's black and isn't even a flip phone.

"This one?" Even Jeffrey seems doubtful.

"It's cute," my mom says.

"Uh, no," I say. "I want the purple one." She's lucky I'm not asking for an iPhone. Or one of those phones that doubles as a personal computer. All I want is a very standard purple phone with a slide out screen. Ooooh, and some sparkly jewels to decorate it with. I slide the package off the rack and place it on the counter.

My mom looks down and sighs. "Wrap it up," she tells Jeffrey.

On our way out the door, while I'm happily swinging my package (my new phone isn't charged, which means I can't use it right away, what's up with that?), my mom says, "Devon, about Luke—"

"Yes, Mr. President, I am on my way!" Katie says from behind us. I turn around to see her still holding the sample phone she was using in the store.

"Katie!" my mom yells. "You stole that phone!"

"No, I didn't," Katie says, sounding haughty. "It is a sample. A free sample for the customers!"

"Oh, God," I say. "You're lucky you didn't set off the alarm going out of the store with that thing."

Katie's eyes widen in horror.

"Come on," my mom says, taking Katie's hand. "We have to bring this back."

"I'll wait here," I say, opening the car door. I want to play with my new phone, even if it's not working just yet.

"Don't think I forgot about Luke," my mom says. "And we *will* be talking about it later." Great.

⊚ ⊚ ⊚

But by the time Saturday rolls around, my mom still hasn't brought up the Luke situation. I am not fooled by this, though. She is probably discussing it with my dad, and they are just waiting for the perfect time to bombard me with it.

But whatevs. Honestly, I have bigger problems. Like the fact that Lexi and her mom are supposed to be picking me up so we can go to Bailey's party, and they are twenty minutes late. Twenty minutes is *way* beyond being fashionably late, and besides, I don't *want* to be late. Not at all. Twenty minutes late is twenty minutes that Luke is probably there, hanging out with Bailey. Twenty minutes that they could be starting up a game of spin the bottle. Twenty minutes that they could be deciding how bad they want to get back together.

You'd think that he would have wanted to drive over to the party with me, his girlfriend, but nooo. "Don't worry about it," he said. "I can get my dad to drive me." Even when I pointed out that it was no big deal, that Lexi's mom would be happy to pick him up, he still didn't get it. He said that his mom would take him and Jared, and they would just meet us there.

The other reason I'm freaking out? Lexi and her mom were supposed to be picking up Greg/Ryan before they came to get me. I wanted to go for the ride, and have Lexi's mom pick up Greg AFTER she picked me up—I figured that way, I'd be able to get to know him in the car a little bit, in case anyone asked us any hard questions. But nooo. Lexi's mom said that was too inconvenient for her. I know I should be thankful that her mom is even picking him up at all, since he lives over an hour away. But it's not like she has anything better to do. And besides, Mrs. Cortland totally hates me. She thinks I'm not good enough for Lexi to hang out with. She's never come out and said this, but I can tell by the way she looks at me. And my outfits.

Although I can't imagine she'll be too upset when she sees me today. I look fab, if I do say so myself. I'm wearing a DKNY crimson sweater over skinny jeans I borrowed from Lexi. I also borrowed (without her knowledge, but it still counts as borrowing, because I'm totally going to give them back) my mom's black boots from her closet. I look *very* grown-up. And yeah, the sweater is last season (back when my parents were feeling guilty about sending me to my grandma's for the summer and so they were giving me whatever I wanted), but it's not like anyone's going to notice.

I check the clock over the living room couch and look out the window again. Where are they? They better hurry up. My mom's in the kitchen working on her computer, and if she comes out here and sees me wearing her boots, I'll be in trouble. Plus I don't have any other shoes that go with this outfit. Obviously the best thing to do would be to put the boots on when I got into the car, but since Ryan/Greg is going to be there, this isn't really an option. Too embarrassing.

I'm just about to call Lexi on my cell to see what's taking so long, when Mrs. Cortland's Hummer pulls into the driveway. Score! I've never ridden in the Hummer before.

I hop (well, okay, fine, sort of stumble and slide— these boots are too tight) out of the house and down the steps without saying goodbye to my mom. Oopsies. I open the back passenger side door, and get ready to haul myself into the car. But there's already someone there. A guy. Ryan/Greg, I suppose.

"Oh," I say. "Sorry, I'll go around."

"No problem, babe," he says. And then he jumps out of the car, walks around to the other side, and opens the door for me. I'm a little startled. Is he for real? "Babe"? Opening car doors for me? But what can I do? I follow him around to the other side of the car, and hop in.

chapter seven

"Now," Lexi says. "Remember that Bailey is totally mean, and you shouldn't be taken in by her, even for a second. Okay, Ryan?"

"Okay," he says. He sounds confident. I peek over at him out of the corner of my eye. Long eyelashes, dark jeans. He's wearing a red Quiksilver T-shirt under a plain brown zip-up sweatshirt. New sneakers (but not too new—they're slightly dirty, like he's been out playing sports or something), and a silver chain around his neck complete the look. Lexi was right—he's pretty cute. Exactly what I need to let Bailey know I'm a force to be reckoned with.

"This is going to be really fun." Lexi leans over the seat and holds out the bag of popcorn that she's been munching on. "Want some?"

"No thanks," I say. My stomach is turning, I'm so nervous. I can't even think about eating. Ryan/Greg takes a big handful and munches on it noisily. Hmm. He's not the neatest eater. I should probably keep him away from the snack table.

"Alexis, is that popcorn?" Mrs. Cortland asks. "You know you're not supposed to be eating popcorn with your braces."

"It's not popcorn," Lexi lies. "Is it, Devi?"

"No," I mumble. Lexi's mom glances at me in the rearview mirror.

"I like your sweater, Devon," she says.

"Thank you," I say. Wow. Lexi's mom is actually being nice to me.

"DKNY, right? Last season?"

"Yeah." So much for her being nice. Greg/Ryan must notice the look on my face, because he does something totally weird. He reaches over and squeezes my hand! Right there in the car, like it's the most natural thing in the world! And then he leans over and whispers into my ear, "Ahh, don't let her get to you. She can be a bit much, but she has a good heart." Then he *squeezes my hand again,* and returns to the other side of the car.

Ohmigod. Ohmigod, ohmigod. Squeezing my hand? Is that cheating? Am I cheating on Luke? Is Greg/Ryan going to start taking his role a little too far? I eye him warily.

"Now, you two should get to know each other," Lexi rambles on from the front seat, obviously oblivious to the fact that very scandalous hand-squeezing is going on back here. "So that there's no confusion when we get to the party."

My hand feels hot. I look down at it, almost expecting it to be red, with big black letters that say CHEATER LIAR. But it looks exactly the same. I take a deep breath. No big deal. He just squeezed my hand. There's nothing wrong with that. I squeeze Mel's hand all the time. Well, not really. But if I did, it wouldn't be cheating. It would just be one friend, squeezing another friend's hand.

"So, uh, Greg," I say, wiping my hand on my jeans. "Do you have any brothers or sisters?"

Lexi, looking satisfied, turns back toward the front of the car and starts talking to her mom about how many calories are in a bag of popcorn. If Mrs. Cortland is wondering what sort of plan Lexi and I have cooked up, she doesn't show it. She doesn't seem interested in the least.

"Two brothers," Greg/Ryan says. "Tim and Kyle."

Tim and Kyle. Right. I can remember that. Easy peasy. Although . . .

"Actually," I say. "It might be better if we didn't use your real life."

"What do you mean?" he asks. He's looking right into my eyes, and it makes me a little nervous after all the crazy hand squeezing that was going on.

"Well, I might not be able to remember everything you tell me," I say. "But if I just make it up . . ."

"Right," he says. "If you just make it up, then it won't matter. Good idea."

"Exactly," I breathe a sigh of relief. Okay, Devon, I think. This is going to be easy. You just have to get through this party, and then send Greg/Ryan on his way. "Also, you have to remember that your name is Ryan. I mean, Greg." Shoot. This is already getting confusing.

"Of course," he says. He leans back in his seat, looking as cool as a cucumber. Why wouldn't he be? It's not his social future that's on the line. Oh, why, oh, why am I always getting myself into these messes?

"Oh, and remember that we dated this summer, and that we met because—"

"Devon," he says, looking me straight in the eye again. "Just relax." And then he squeezes my hand again.

"Now, make sure you act happy," Lexi says. She's clattering up the pathway to Bailey Barelli's house, her high shoes making noises on the cobblestone walk. I'm rushing to keep up with her, in my mom's boots.

"I don't have to act happy," I say. "I *am* happy." Lie, lie, lie. Greg/Ryan grins at me, like he's the reason I'm happy. Ugh. I do want him to seem like he likes me, but not so much that it's weird. I already feel guilty for all the hand squeezing.

Maybe I should say something to him. Just a little something. Like, "Hey, Greg, you seem cool and all, but let's not take this too far, you know?" But what if he gets mad? Besides, I'm sure it will be fine. I'm sure he's going to be totally cool. Nothing bad's going to happen. In fact, it's going to be great. I plaster a huge smile on my face.

Lexi rings the doorbell.

Suddenly, my feet slip on Bailey's front porch, and the heel of my boot bends to the side. Ouch. I right myself, but then the other boot gets a little off balance, and the next thing I know, my arms are flailing and I'm about to fall flat on my face. "Whoa, whoa, whoa," I screech, my arms spinning in circles as I try to keep my balance. I reach out and attempt to grab the wooden railing of the porch, but it's too far away. The next thing I know, I feel strong arms around me from behind. Greg/Ryan has caught me.

Bailey Barelli chooses that moment to open the door, and when she does, she sees Lexi standing there, and me, splayed across her front porch and gazing up at Greg, who is holding me from behind.

"Oh, hi," she says, grinning. "We were wondering if you two were ever going to get here." From behind her, the sound of music and voices comes wafting out of the house. "You must be Greg," she says. "Hi, I'm Bailey." She giggles. "I'd offer you my hand, but you seem a little tied up."

Greg smiles his perfect smile, and I disentangle myself from his grasp. But not before I look over Bailey's shoulder into the house, and lock eyes with Luke.

Whatever. All Greg/Ryan did was catch me. I mean, I could have *died* if it weren't for him. Slipping and falling can be totally serious. That's how my grandma broke her hip. And one of my mom's friends fell once and got a gaping head wound. So Luke should be *happy* that Greg/Ryan saved my life. And besides, with all the convert note passing that's been going on lately, perhaps those in glass houses shouldn't throw stones.

Not that Luke's said anything. But I can tell he's kind of mad. He shook Greg/Ryan's hand very quickly once we got into the house, and ever since then, he's been glued to my side. Which is good, because Bailey is being super annoying, and trying to get everyone to dance. And when I say everyone, I mean Luke. She's put on some fast music, and now she's in the middle of her family room, dancing around like a crazy person. Every so often, she'll go, "Come on, you guys, you have to dance with me!" And then she tries to pull on Luke's hand, but he won't go.

"So," he says. We're leaning back on the couch, and he has his arm around me. "Are you excited for the dance?"

"Super excited," I say, watching Greg/Ryan out of the corner of my eye. He's over in the corner with Lexi and Jared, and some girl from our science class. I'm hoping he won't go for the chips that are sitting on the table, what with his messy eating habits and all. "Lexi and I are going shopping for stuff to wear. And do you want to ride over with them in the Hummer? Lexi has this whole thing planned. She's kind of making a big deal about it."

"Sure," Luke says, smiling down at me. "So your mom's cool with it then?"

"Welll," I say, "not exactly."

"What does 'not exactly' mean, exactly?"

"It means she said I could go to the dance, but I haven't exactly told her I'm going with you."

"Oh." Luke shifts on the couch and looks straight ahead. In front of us, Bailey is doing some crazy dance move, all the while watching us out of the corner of her eye. She's wearing a dark purple party dress with a flared bottom and a layer of dark purple glittery ribbing all around the bottom. She's also wearing glittery purple eye shadow.

"Oh? Are you annoyed or something?"

"No," Luke sighs. Okay then. "It's just . . . I don't understand what the big deal is about telling your family about me."

"Nothing," I say. "There is no big deal. Unless you count the fact that my mom would freak out if she knew you and I were together."

"I don't think she would," Luke says.

I stare at him blankly. "Do you not remember when you came over to my house, and my mom caught you there and flipped out?"

"Your mom flipped out because you weren't supposed

to be having friends over while you were babysitting."

"Nooo," I say. "My mom flipped out because she is very strict. Ridiculously strict."

"Look, all I'm saying is that maybe you should tell her. She might be okay with it, if you were honest from the start." He pulls his arm out from around me, totally ruining my snuggling. I stare at him blankly. Are we having a fight? Is Luke giving me an ultimatum? Tell your parents or else?

"If I were honest from the start? What's that supposed to mean?"

"Nothing," he says. But he's not looking at me. What the heck is going on here?

"Hey, babe," Greg/Ryan says, appearing in front of us. He's holding two plastic cups of soda, and he hands me one. "I thought you might be thirsty."

I take one of the cups. "Thanks," I say. I take a sip of the soda. Eww. Sprite. I don't like Sprite. I prefer to keep my soft drinks limited to those in the cola family, thank you very much.

Luke notices the face I'm making, and he looks into my cup. "Sprite?" he says, frowning. "You hate Sprite."

"It's a, uh, a private joke," I say. I smile and take another sip. It's not that bad. I'm getting used to it. Mmm. Nice, sparkling lemon-lime flavor.

"A private joke?" Luke looks dubious.

"Yeah, see, we used to make our own soda over the summer," I say, laughing. I telegraph to Greg with my eyes that he better laugh, too. He figures it out and lets out a good chuckle.

"Yeah, and Devon used to always love the lemon-lime I made her, she said it was the best soda she'd ever tasted because it was made with love."

Oh, geez. Not the thing to say, Greg/Ryan. But I just smile and take another sip of my soda. Luke looks like maybe he's about to reach over and wring Greg/Ryan's neck.

"Oh, hi, guys," Kim says, sauntering up to us. "I see you got here early." She's wearing a tight black mini-skirt over red and black patterned tights, and a red lacy shirt. Her hair is swept up into an updo. She looks absolutely fabulous.

And anyway, we were actually twenty minutes *late*. But leave it to Kim to be *thirty* minutes late, making us look like the losers who showed up early. "And you must be Greg." She holds out her hand, and Greg/Ryan goes to shake it. But at the last second, she moves it toward his mouth, and basically forces him to kiss her hand. Eww.

"What's everyone doing? Dancing?" She looks at

Greg/Ryan, then leans in close to him. Probably so he can smell her perfume. "Do you want to dance?"

I try to telegraph to him that no, this is not a good idea, but this time, he doesn't seem to get the message. I'm not sure if he thinks I want him to dance with Kim, or if he's just taken in by how cute she is. Probably the cute thing. She takes his hand and leads him off, and then Luke looks at me.

"Well, that was pretty obvious," he says.

"You thought so, too?" I say. "I mean, obviously she just wanted to dance with him to make me jealous. I mean, look at those two." In the middle of Bailey Barelli's family room, Bailey and Kim are now both dancing with Greg. He's actually a pretty good dancer.

"I wasn't talking about them," Luke says, looking grim.

"What were you talking about?" Please don't say it's obvious I never met Greg until this morning, please don't say it's obvious I . . .

"That Greg still likes you." Um. Uh-oh.

"What? No, I mean, that's absolutely ridiculous. We're just friends."

"Friends who call each other 'babe'? Devon, I saw him holding you when Bailey opened the front door."

"What? No, I was about to fall." I hold up my

crazy boots to illustrate the point. "See? I'm wearing completely ridiculous and inappropriate boots that I stole from my mother."

At that moment, Mel comes wandering into Bailey's family room, looking confused.

"There you are!" she says when she spots me. "I've been ringing the doorbell forever, but no one came. So finally I just walked in."

"I guess no one could hear it with all the music going on." Mel looks out onto the dance floor, where Bailey and Kim are basically doing a pole dance around Greg.

"Is that Greg?" Mel sounds doubtful.

"Yup," I say. "That's Greg. My *ex*-boyfriend. Who I'm totally over." I raise my voice a little so that Luke will be sure to hear. "And who's obviously totally over me, since he's out there dancing with two other girls."

"Oh, please," Luke scoffs. "It's obvious that he's dancing with them just to make you jealous." He drains the rest of the soda that's in his cup. "I'm going to get another drink," he says. "Do you want anything?"

"No," I say. "I'm good." I take a sip of my Sprite.

"Right," he says, walking off.

"No, wait, actually, I mean I'd like a Coke!" I yell after him. But he doesn't hear me. Either that, or he just doesn't want to listen. Mel and I watch as he walks over to the table where the drinks are, pours himself a cup of soda, and then starts talking to Lexi and Jared. He doesn't seem like he's in too much of a hurry to get back over to me.

"Wow," Mel says. "What did I miss?"

"Isn't it obvious?" I say. "It's a complete and total disaster." I sit back down on the couch, and Mel slides down next to me. For the first time, I notice Mel's all dressed up. And not in the going-to-a-party-at-Bailey-Barelli's kind of way, but more of a going-to-church-and-or-my-grandma's-house kind of way. She's wearing a long black dress and black flats, and her hair is pulled back into a neat bun. "Why are you all dressed up?" I asked her.

"I just felt like it," Mel says, looking down at the floor. I frown. Lexi and I offered to give Mel a ride over here with us, but she turned it down, saying that her mom would drive her. It seemed a little weird at the time, but I was so consumed with what was going to happen at the party, that I didn't really think too much about it. But now it seems *very* weird.

"Okay," I say, crossing my arms. "What's going on?"

"What do you mean?" She tries to look innocent, but I'm not buying it. Her eyes flutter over to the soda table. "Do they have iced tea over there? I could really use a drink."

"Don't try to change the subject," I say. I stand up, grab her hand, and march her into the hallway outside of Bailey's family room. The walls there are covered with pictures of Bailey and her sister. Bailey on a beach, Bailey in second grade, Bailey, Bailey, Bailey. I resist the urge to study some of the group shots up close, to see if Luke is in any of them. "Spill."

"There's nothing going on," she says. Her eyes are darting around nervously, like she's some kind of animal that I have cornered.

"I don't believe you," I challenge. "You've been acting weird for the past week. There was that paper that fell out of your locker, and how you didn't want me and Lexi to stay for dinner, and how you didn't want to ride over here with us." She doesn't say anything, and just bites her lip. "And then when you do show up, you're dressed like you've been . . . I dunno, at some kind of college interview or something." I expect her to laugh, but a look of panic flashes across her face.

"That's crazy." She forces a laugh.

"Is it?"

She slides down the wall and collapses into a heap on the floor of Bailey Barelli's front hallway. Her dress makes a pool around her knees, and she looks like she's floating in a sea of black skirt.

"What is it?" I ask. I try to get down next to her, but my jeans won't really let me. So I settle for crouching, but that doesn't really work either, because of my boots. Finally, I give up and just plop down on my butt, sprawling out next to her.

And then I notice that Mel is crying. A big tear slides down her cheek and lands on the floor.

"What is it?" I repeat. "Mel, what's wrong?" Then I realize I've never seen Mel wear all black before. "Were you . . . were you at a funeral?" Mel is very close to her Grandma Purvis, her dad's mom. Maybe she's been sick or something, and Mel didn't want to tell me because she didn't want me to worry. And now I've made her come all the way out here to stupid Bailey Barelli's house, so that she could provide moral support because of my stupid fake boyfriend situation. I should be ashamed of myself.

"No," Mel says. She wipes at her eyes with the back of her hand. "No one died."

Oh. Phew. "Then what is it? Does it have to do with Dylan? What did that jerk do? I swear to God I'll—"

"No," Mel says. "It's not Dylan." Oh. Right. Why

would Dylan make Mel dress all in black? Unless she was in mourning for him or something. But that's ridiculous. Obviously I'm not a very good guesser. So I decide to just wait. I mean, Mel will tell me, right? And if she doesn't want to, then I have to respect that. I'll be hurt, of course, but a girl has to have some—

"Private school," Mel whispers. She looks up at me, her eyes watery, like two dark pools.

"Private school? Ooh," I say, nodding. "Does this have anything to do with those two girls who live down the street from you?" There are these two totally obnoxious girls who live a few doors down from Mel—I can never remember their names, Cyn and Win, or something. They're twins. Anyway, they go to private school and are super snotty. Sometimes they make fun of Mel, and one time, when we were in fourth grade, they wrote "Mel Smells" on her driveway in chalk. Super mature, that Cyn and Win. "Are they giving you a hard time again? Don't worry about it, we'll get Lexi to come over and talk to them." Lexi's very tough. Most people are scared of her, especially when she gets really angry.

"Devon," Mel says. She grabs my shoulders. "This has nothing to do with Molly and Polly." Aha! Molly and Polly! I should have remembered, since Polly totally sounds like a parrot when she talks.

"Then what does it have to do with private school?"

"My mom wants me to go," she says, shrugging. "To private school. Starting this year. Soon. As soon as she can get me in."

"What?!" I'm so shocked that if I weren't already sprawled in Bailey's hallway, I probably would have fallen over. "What do you mean, your mom wants you to go to private school?"

"My mom wants me to go to private school," Mel repeats, speaking slowly so I'll understand.

"But *why*?" Private school sounds horrible. Uniforms. Girls like Cyn and Win. Tons of homework. And no BFF, i.e., me.

"She thinks I'd do better if I was in a different academic environment," Mel says. "She thinks that since I'm only a few years away from high school, I really need to start focusing on school so that I can get into a good college."

"But can't you just focus on school at our school?" I'm starting to know what people mean when they say they're having a panic attack. My heart is in my chest, and the room feels very, very small. Of course, that could be because we're sitting in a very small hallway, but still. I can't even imagine not being in school with Mel. Not dropping off our notebook in her locker every day. Not eating lunch with her. Not meeting her before class. Not talking to her during science. What if she makes a new best friend? A new, cooler, private-school best friend, and she forgets all about me? I feel a lump rise in my throat.

"Not according to my mom," Mel says. "Devon, what am I going to do? At first I thought she was just sort of messing around with the idea, you know?" She sniffles. "But now she's actually taking it seriously. The reason I'm dressed up is because I had an admissions interview this morning." She sniffs again, and I stand up and head into Barelli's downstairs bathroom to get Mel a tissue.

"Here," I say, giving Mel her tissue. She wipes her nose, and then hiccups.

"What am I going to do?" she says again.

"Don't worry," I say, giving her a hug. "We'll figure it out."

"But *how*?" Mel wails.

Greg/Ryan pops his head around the wall, and peers into the bathroom, obviously not caring that it might be slightly inappropriate to look into a bathroom when someone's in it. Even if we did leave the door open. "There you are, babe," he says. "I've been looking all over for you."

And then it hits me. The perfect way to keep Mel out of private school. "Hey, Greg," I say. "What are you doing next weekend?"

By the time the party is over, I still haven't figured things out with Luke. He was perfectly nice to me for the rest of the party, but we ended up sitting in a group for most of the time, hanging out with everyone. And not really talking just to each other. Although at one point, when Mel, Greg/Ryan and I got back from the bathroom, Luke said, "Where were you?" and I said, "Talking to Mel." Which was true. But Luke obviously knew that Greg/Ryan followed us.

And I can't tell him that we were hatching a plan to get Greg back here next weekend, so that he can pretend to be a student at St. Mary's, the private school Mel's mom wants to send her to. We figured out that if we can get Greg/Ryan to act all crazy in front of her, then maybe Mel's mom will see that boarding school isn't the right place for her after all.

"You should totally grow a mustache," Lexi says from the front seat when we're on our way home in her mom's car. "You would look so hard-core."

Mrs. Cortland doesn't even react. Maybe she didn't hear, since she's on some kind of business call. She's talking into her cell phone headset. At least, supposedly it's a business call. All I've heard her do so far is make plans to meet whoever it is she's talking to for lunch and a pedicure. Lexi's mom has her own real estate business, and Lexi says a lot of her mom's work is networking with the right people. So maybe that's why she has to go out for manicures a lot.

"A mustache?" I ask, not convinced. I look at Greg/Ryan's face where he's sitting next to me in the car. He doesn't look like he could grow a whisker, much less a full mustache.

"Good idea," Greg says. He strokes his chin thoughtfully.

"Anyway, you can't go too overboard," I say. "You have to make it believable."

"Yeah, like you can't freak her out too much," Lexi says. "You just have to make the mom think that you shouldn't be going to school with her innocent daughter."

"Ladies," Greg/Ryan says, leaning back in the seat. He drapes his arms over the back of the seat and gives me a smile. "Wasn't I good in the role of Devon's boyfriend?" He looks at me and winks. "Just trust me."

Right.

I have to make sure to keep my hands in my lap so that there's no scandalous hand squeezing, but I never thought about him trying to put his arm around me. Not that that's what he's doing exactly, but close enough. What if he tries to squeeze my shoulder? Is shoulder squeezing better or worse than hand squeezing?

I feel my cell phone start to vibrate in my purse, and I pull it out. Yay! It's probably a text from Luke! Saying he's sorry that we had such a weird party, and that he'll see me tomorrow, when we get together to go over some mock trial stuff. And then maybe he'll sign it with a little heart, like he sometimes does. But it's not Luke. It's my mom. When did my mom learn to text? I hope this doesn't mean she's going to be texting me all the time. So not cool.

"When will you be home?" it says.

"Two minutes," I reply, and then shove my phone back into my bag.

When we pull up in front of my house, I thank Mrs. Cortland for the ride, and tell Lexi to call me later. "Uh, nice meeting you, Greg," I say. "Um, Ryan."

"Nice meeting you, too, Devi," he says. He reaches over and grabs me in a hug. Um, eww. He smells nice, though. Like soap and clean clothes. I pull away and disentangle myself from his arms (awwwk-waard), and I'm just about to open the car door when I catch sight of my mom coming out of our house.

Her hair's swept up in a messy bun, with lots of little tendrils falling out, and she's wearing jeans and a black sweater with a dishtowel thrown over her shoulder.

"Hiii," she calls, waving as she steps through the piles of leaves on our lawn. The dishtowel falls to the ground, but she doesn't seem to notice.

She rushes right up to the car and over to the driver's side window. Mrs. Cortland looks at her like she's crazy as my mom motions for her to roll down the window. Yikes. I hope she didn't see me hugging Greg.

"Hi," my mom says once Lexi's mom has ended her phone call and has rolled down the window. "I'm Marcia Delaney, Devon's mom."

"Hi," Lexi's mom says.

"Hi, Mrs. Delaney!" Lexi yells from the passenger seat.

"Hello, Lexi," my mom says. "Don't you look nice."

"Thank you." Lexi preens, and my mom peers into the backseat.

"Oh," she says. "And who's this young man back

there with Devon?" She says it in a light tone, but I know enough to realize she wants to know exactly who he is, and uh, what he's doing in the backseat with me.

"Oh, that's just Greg," Lexi says, waving her hand as if he's no one. "Just a friend from my old school. Him and Devon don't even know each other."

"Nice to meet you," Greg/Ryan says. He gives my mom a little signal of salute with his fingers, which is weird, but my mom seems to like it. "You can call me Ryan." My mom frowns.

"So," Lexi's mom says. She leans her hand against the steering wheel and slides her big Paris Hilton sunglasses down over her eyes. Even though it's not really that sunny out. "It was nice to meet you."

My mom gets thrown for a second, but recovers quickly. "Actually, I was hoping we could talk for a second. I'm sorry, what did you say your name was?"

"Diane," Mrs. Cortland says.

"Diane," my mom replies. "I wanted to touch base with you about the dance that's coming up at school."

Mrs. Cortland looks at my mom blankly. "The dance?" she asks.

"Yes," my mom says. "The one the girls are planning on going to."

"There's a dance at school next week," Lexi says.

"Remember? You said we could go in the Hummer." She squeals. "Not to mention the pre- and post-parties, holla!"

Not the best thing to say in front of my mom. I don't think she looks too fondly upon pre- and post-parties, or upon the word "holla."

"Woot, woot," Greg/Ryan chimes in. He grins at me.

"Oh, right," Mrs. Cortland says. "It should be fun." She looks into the backseat at me. "It was nice to see you, Devon." Right. It's obvious she wants me to get out of the car. Then I realize I'm still wearing my mom's boots. Crap. I was planning on ditching them in the garage on my way into the house, but now I obviously won't be able to do that, since I'll be walking right by my mom.

Hmm. I wonder if I can wiggle out of them, and somehow leave them in Lexi's car, hop into the house without my mom realizing that I'm not wearing any shoes, and then pick them up later. I reach down and slowly start pulling the zipper of the left boot down toward the heel.

"Yes, well, I'm assuming that these pre- and post-parties you're planning will be supervised," my mom says.

"Of course," Mrs. Cortland replies. But she doesn't

really seem like she's that interested or even means it. Which she probably doesn't. I've hung out at Lexi's house a lot, and her mom is hardly ever there. She's always either out working, or in her workout room, or just . . . I don't know. Out. Lexi's dad is never home. He's always on business trips. He sends Lexi soaps and chocolates from all these different countries.

"And will there be boys attending?" my mom persists.

Ohmigod. I want to die. *Will there be boys attending?* Who asks that? And what is wrong with this boot? The zipper is not even moving at all. Have my feet gotten bigger within the past few hours? It must be all this stress. It's causing my feet to swell. Definitely not good. I finally slide the zipper all the way down, and pull my foot out of the boot. Ahh.

"The party? Or the dance?" Lexi's mom asks.

"The party," my mom says.

"Well, I'm sure the girls will have their dates there," Lexi's mom says.

"Oh." My mom looks a little shocked. "I wasn't aware that the girls would be going with dates."

"Well, it is, you know, *customary* for them to go to the dance with their boyfriends. Lexi will go with Jared, and Devon will go with Luke, and I suppose whatever other friends they have going with them will wander into the party."

The other boot comes off, and I very casually slide it under the seat in front of me. No sweat. Now all I have to do is make it into the house without my mom noticing that I'm in bare feet. Which actually doesn't seem like it's going to be a very hard thing to do, since she is getting very angry. I can tell because she says, "Is that so?" to Lexi's mom. My mom only says "is that so?" to people when she's extremely mad. And although she's saying it to Lexi's mom, it's also about me. And the fact that I have a date for the dance and haven't really told her.

"Well," I say loudly. "I guess I'll see you guys later!" I open the back door of the car. "Bye, Lex! Bye, Greg!"

"Bye," they both say.

When I get out of the car and over to where my mom is standing in the driveway, I have to pretty much grab her and pull her away from Lexi's mom's car. But she kind of has no choice, because Lexi's mom's phone has rung, and she's picked it up and is talking into it. I guess she's done talking to my mom. Yikes.

"That woman is so rude!" my mom says as I lead her toward the house.

"Totally," I say. I never realized how cold the cobblestone walk leading up to our front door is. Probably because I don't ever walk on it in bare feet, except in summer. And then it's obviously hot. I'm basically hopping up the walk, and hoping my mom doesn't notice. But since she's so mad, she doesn't seem to.

And then, right when we're about to open the door, Lexi's mom honks the horn of the Hummer. And when we turn around, Greg/Ryan is leaning out the car window, waving my mom's boot in the air.

"Hey, Devon," he says, grinning. "Your forgot your shoes!"

chapter eight

Okay. So. She can't get too mad at me for taking her shoes. I mean, they're just shoes.

The whole boyfriend thing is another matter. She's definitely going to be mad about that. Right now she is making us grilled cheese sandwiches, which is not a good sign. When my mom gets mad, she just yells and grounds me like a normal mom. When she gets really mad, and there's some kind of life issue she feels we need to discuss, she gets rid of my dad and Katie, and talks to me alone. And makes us food.

"We are going to the grocery store," Katie sings, dancing into the kitchen, where I'm sitting at the kitchen table, drinking a glass of chocolate milk. "I'm going with Daddy, and you cannot go."

"Great," I say.

"But don't worry. I am going to get you a present of one chocolate bar!"

I don't say anything.

"I said," Katie repeats, "that I am going to get you a present of one chocolate bar!"

"Thank you, Katie," I say. "That is very kind of you."

Katie beams.

"Where's the list?" my dad asks, walking into the kitchen. He pulls his cell phone off the charger on the counter and slips it into his pocket. Hmm. Very suspicious. He probably wants to call his girlfriend while he's out with Katie. The thought of this makes my throat get all tight, and it just keeps getting tighter and tighter, and by the time Katie and my dad walk out the door a few minutes later, tears are threatening to spill down my cheeks.

My mom places a plate of grilled cheese sandwiches in front of me, cut in half diagonally just the way I like it, and I burst into tears. She looks shocked.

"There's no need to cry about it, Devon," she says. "They're just boots, I'm not that mad."

"No," I say between sniffles. "It's not that." I blow my nose on my napkin.

"Then what is it?" she asks. She puts a cup of tea down in front of her own plate, and sits down at the table with me.

"Nothing," I mumble, swiping at my tears with the back of my hand. How can I tell her that while she's here making grilled cheese sandwiches and cutting them in half like she knows I like, my dad is out with my little sister probably making phone calls to some other woman? And how could I have taken her boots? She's going to need them if she becomes single again.

"Devon, we need to talk about Luke," my mom says.

"I'm so sorry I didn't tell you," I say. I blow my nose again and then take a tiny bit of my grilled cheese, which makes me feel a little bit better. "I just didn't want you to freak out."

"So he is your boyfriend then?"

"Yes," I say.

"And what does that mean to you, exactly, having a boyfriend?" she asks.

"Um, I don't know. That we talk on the phone and maybe hold hands at school and go to the dance together and I'm not allowed to do that with any other boys."

My mom looks relieved. I guess she thought maybe I was a step away from ending up married with children. I mean, we haven't even French kissed yet. Lexi and Jared do it all the time, and her mom doesn't even seem concerned about it. Thinking of French kissing Luke starts to make me feel hot all over, and I take a sip of the cool milk, hoping it will calm me down.

"Devon, you know it's okay for you to be interested in boys. What I don't like is the sneaking around." She wipes her mouth with her napkin and looks thoughtful.

My cell phone starts ringing, and I look at the caller ID and see Luke's name blinking. Yay! He can't be too mad if he's calling, right? Thank God Lexi didn't change my phone so that it would say "my1&only" like she threatened to the other day when she was setting up a ringtone for me. I don't think my mom would take too kindly to that, and our talk is going so well. She's not even that mad about the boots!

"Who's that?" she asks, trying to look nonchalant.

"It's Luke," I say, holding it up and showing her, so that she won't think I'm trying to hide stuff from her.

"I'm just going to answer it and tell him I'll call him back, is that okay?"

"Of course," she says. But the look on her face says maybe she's still a little freaked out. But I will show her there's nothing to freak out about, that there's nothing going on here, just an innocent little junior high school romance. Well, not exactly that innocent. With the fake ex-boyfriends and all. La, la-la.

"Hey," I say, flipping open my phone.

"Hi," Luke says. And he doesn't sound too friendly. I guess he *is* still mad about the party, and about Greg/Ryan. Thank God he won't be coming around again. Greg/Ryan, I mean. Well, except for next weekend when he plays a troubled kid from the wrong side of the tracks who goes to St. Mary's. But Luke doesn't need to know about that.

"What's up? I'm just having a grilled cheese with my mom. She cut it in half just the way I like it," I tell him, glancing at my mom out of the corner of my eye, and hoping this will score points with her.

"Fun," he says, but he doesn't sound like he really means it. "Listen, I think we should talk about what happened at the party. You know, uh, with Greg." I chew slowly on my grilled cheese.

"Welll," I say, wondering just how I'm going to be

able to talk about Greg/Ryan when my mom is sitting right next to me. Also, why is Luke bringing this up, anyway? As far as I'm concerned, Greg/Ryan is over. He doesn't affect our lives anymore. He's just, poof, gone! I wonder if maybe I should make him move away? Or give him some kind of incurable disease? "I don't know what there is to talk about."

"How about how you basically ignored me so that you could have a secret conference with him and Mel?"

"No, I didn't," I say.

"Yes, you did," he says. "And you don't even sound that upset about it."

"I am," I say.

"You don't sound it."

"Well, it's hard right now, since I'm, you know, eating this grilled cheese and all." I hope he realizes that *eating this grilled cheese* is code for *my mom is right here so I can't talk about this stuff*, but Luke apparently doesn't get it.

"You still haven't told your mom about me?" he asks.

"Yes, actually, I have," I say, proud of myself. I take a bite of my grilled cheese, chew, swallow, and take a swig of milk. No sweat.

"Then why are you still being so secretive?" he wants to know.

"You're right, we should totally talk about that in mock trial tomorrow," I say. Hopefully he knows this means, *We're in the middle of talking about you right now and we'll talk about this tomorrow*, while my mom will interpret it to mean that Luke is so obviously smart that he's the one who wanted me to get into mock trial, a very valuable extracurricular that will allow me to get into the college of my choice.

"In mock trial tomorrow?" Luke asks. "Why would we talk about this in mock trial?"

"Because that would be cool," I say. My mom is chewing on her sandwich and looking at something on the wall, squinting at one of our pictures like maybe she's thinking it needs to be replaced or something. But I know she's just doing that so it won't seem like she's listening to my conversation. "So maybe I'll call you back later?"

"Devon," Luke says, his voice getting all soft. "Look, I'm sorry if I'm freaking out about this. But I miss you."

My face flushes and my stomach does a huge flip. He misses me! Even though he just saw me a couple of hours ago, he misses me! But of course I can't say that back. So I just say, "See you tomorrow, too," and then I flip my phone shut.

"Maybe you should have Luke over for dinner tomorrow," my mom says.

"Maybe I should," I say.

She changes the subject then, and we talk about Katie being obsessed with the whole Olympic scandal, and how she wants to get her hair cut. We don't talk that much about Luke, and I can tell my mom is trying to be cool about it.But later, when I'm alone in my room, I call Luke back on my cell so I can tell him I miss him, too. But he never answers, and by the time I fall asleep, he hasn't called me back.

"Look, you're going to have to do it sometime," Lexi says to Mel.

"That's not true!" Mel says. "I can definitely decide not to do it ever. Ever in my life." She looks a little green. Although it could be the shirt she's wearing, a yellow, long-sleeved T-shirt that says "Peace" in bubbly black letters. I keep telling her not to wear yellow with her skin tone, but does she listen to me? Nooo. Of course, it could also be the lighting here, too. The hallway at school is very unforgiving and does not do anything for anyone's complexion. Well, except Bailey Barelli. Her skin always looks flawless.

"Ohmigod, here he comes," I say, and turn back toward Lexi's locker. It's between second and third period on Monday, and Lexi is trying to convince Mel she needs to ask Dylan to the dance. But Mel is resisting. We all hold our breaths as Dylan walks by, and I pretend to be talking about something inside Lexi's locker.

"So that's what your mirror looks like!" I say really loudly as Dylan passes by, my face buried in Lexi's locker.

"Like that wasn't obvious," Lexi sniffs once Dylan's out of earshot. I remove my head from her locker and Lexi slams it shut.

"Excuse me?" I say. "But that was a very good line. I mean, why else would my head have been all the way in your locker if it wasn't to either look at your mirror or avoid Dylan?"

"Anyway," Lexi tells Mel, ignoring my explanation, "I'm not saying you're going to have to ask him out."

Mel smiles.

"But," Lexi goes on, "eventually, at some point, you are going to have to ask a guy out."

"Why?" Mel asks. "Why should I ask a guy out?"

"Because don't you want to be able to go for what you want?" Lexi asks. She pulls on the hem of the super short purple skirt she's wearing over purple tights. My mom would have FREAKED if I'd gone out of the house wearing that. But something tells me Lexi's mom doesn't care. She probably bought it for her.

"Not if what I want doesn't want me," Mel says. She looks satisfied.

"Nothing ventured, nothing gained," I sing. Mel gives me a dirty look.

"All I'm saying," Lexi says. "Is that if you want to ask him out, you should ask him. Besides, it's not fair to expect the guy to do the asking all the time. First, it's extremely sexist and sets the feminist movement back, and second, sometimes guys are shy, too, and you might miss out on someone who really *does* like you just because *he* thinks that *you* don't like him." Lexi snaps her gum.

I'm not sure who's more surprised, me, that Lexi not only knows words like feminist and sexist and is using them correctly, or Mel, because Lexi is making a good case for why she should just ask Dylan to the dance.

The bell rings then, and we all scatter to our classes. Mel looks tortured, so even though I know it's against the rules, I text her from math. "Luv U no matter what." She texts back, "Thx."

Then, since Luke had another dentist appointment this morning and I haven't seen him yet, I decide to send him a text, too, while I'm on my way to my next class. (This information was given to me quite cheerfully by Bailey Barelli, who was just delighted that I didn't know where Luke was. "If you're looking for your boyfriend," she said when she noticed I kept looking at the clock on the wall nervously, "he had a dentist appointment this morning and he won't be here until later." I tried to act like I knew that without actually coming out and saying I knew it, but I'm pretty sure she knew she had the scoop on my boyfriend and I didn't.)

"I miss you, too," I text to Luke. "Hope dentist was okay, see you at lunch."

Immediately, my phone vibrates back, and I reach into my bag to check it. "Dentist was fine," it says. No mention of missing me. Or sitting together at lunch. I start to text him back, but suddenly a hand's on my shoulder, and when I look up, Mr. Ikwang is standing there in the hall.

"No phones in school, Devon," he says cheerfully and holds out his hand. I sigh and place it in his palm.

Mock trial. Bailey Barelli is pretending to be my friend by trying to bond over the fact that Mr. Ikwang took my cell phone. "He totally did that to me, too, at the beginning of the year," she says. "It sucks. Who were you texting with?"

I decide to tell her, and at the same time, get in a little dig. "I was telling Luke how much I missed him, and I just got sort of caught up in the moment, you know?" Then I realize this makes me look like I was chasing him, so I backtrack. "I was just pushing the 2 for the I miss you *too* when—"

"That's so weird, because I was texting with Luke too, when Mr. Ikwang took my phone." Bailey laughs. "Maybe he's bad luck."

"What's bad luck?" Luke asks. He appears next to us, his navy blue book bag slung over his shoulder.

"Texting with you," Bailey says. And then she gives him a poke! A poke! Right on his shoulder, and right in front of me! What is wrong with this girl?

"Why is it bad luck?"

"Because Devon and I both got in trouble when we were texting with you." I don't like when she puts us in the same category, like her texting him is the same as me texting him. I'm his girlfriend. And yeah, things haven't been going the best between us (he spent all of lunch talking to Jared about some dumb sports thing, and I could tell he was still a little mad at me), but we ARE going to the dance together.

"So," I say loudly. "Did you talk to you mom about the dance yet? My mom is sooo excited. Oh, and that reminds me! She wants you to come over for dinner tonight."

"She does?" Luke looks shocked.

"She does?" Bailey looks even more shocked.

"Yes," I say. I run my finger over Luke's palm and then give his hand a squeeze. Until Greg/Ryan squeezed my hand in the car, I never realized just how much one hand squeeze can communicate to someone. "She really wants to meet you. Can you come?"

"Of course," Luke says. "I'll just call my mom after mock trial."

"Good." But suddenly I feel a little uncertain. I mean, I'm sure it will be fine. What could possibly go wrong? It's just a little dinner. Hopefully it will be take-out, though. Not sure how Luke would feel about having to choke down some burned meatloaf or a big pot of greasy stew.

"Your mom must really miss making big meals for everyone," Bailey says, looking fake concerned. She lowers her eyes, and her eyelashes brush against her cheeks.

"What do you mean?" I ask.

"Well, I was talking to Greg at the party, and he was telling me about how he'd always come over to your house and eat dinner with you guys." She smiles. "He said your mom's a great cook, and he'd eat so much that she'd have to make more for everyone."

"Um, yeah," I say. "He loved my mom's cooking." Subject change, subject change! "So what did you guys think about that case we—"

"I thought you said that you dated Greg over the summer, when you were visiting your grandmother." Luke frowns, his eyebrows knitting together in a very cute way. A very cute, confused way that could get me in a lot of trouble.

"I did," I say. "He liked coming over to eat my grandmother's cooking. That's what I meant to say." I smile confidently.

"Nooo," Bailey says. She leans back in her chair and twirls one of her perfect curls around her finger. "He specifically said your mom. I remember."

"Well, that might be because he did come over to our house a couple of times after that summer," I say. "Just to eat a good meal." I open my notebook and pretend to write something down, signaling the conversation is over. But Luke doesn't get it.

"Before or after you broke up?" he wants to know.

"Um, before?" But then I realize that doesn't make sense. "Uh, after, I mean."

"So you guys *are* really good friends then." Luke looks more than a little annoyed, and I can tell Bailey's trying not to smirk. "I mean, if he came over to your house after you broke up."

"We're not friends," I say. "We had a fight, so he didn't come over for a while, and now we're more like acquaintances." I check the clock over the wall. 3:05. Where the heck is Lexi, anyway? She's supposed to be here, offering me moral support. And more importantly, where is Mr. Ikwang? He told me I could have my phone back today, AND he should be starting mock trial, so that we can, you know, mock trials or whatever. Not talk about my fake ex-boyfriends. "You guys had a fight, but then you made up?" Luke asks. What is he, the ex-boyfriend police? Does this mean it's okay for me to start grilling him about the illicit notes and text messages he's been sending to Bailey?

"Yeah," Bailey says helpfully. "He told me at the party the fight was because he still likes you."

I frown. Is this true? And if so, what is *wrong* with Greg/Ryan? Did we not tell him *exactly* what to do at the party? Why would he tell people that he still liked me? He should have been flirting with Kim and Bailey and all the other girls at the party who were cute and wearing short skirts.

"He doesn't still like me," I tell Luke.

"Yes, he does," Bailey says. "He told me."

"No, he doesn't," I say.

"Yes, he does," Bailey says. Then she gets really fake, so fake that I can't believe Luke can't see right through it. "Oh, I'm sorry, I don't mean to cause a fight or anything. I think it's nice that Devon can still be friends with an ex-boyfriend. That means that the two of *you* will be able to be friends someday!"

Mr. Ikwang picks that moment to finally come into the room.

"Sorry I'm late," he says. "Now I have some new packets for you involving a Supreme Court case I think you're just going to love!"

Um, yay?

Yawn. An hour and a half later, I think I might be starting to fall asleep. I've never actually fallen asleep in school before. Although one time last year I did kind of put my head down into my sweater after I finished up a social studies unit test and closed my eyes.

Lexi and Jared never showed up, which means for

the past ninety minutes I've been stuck going over and over a trial with Luke and Bailey. Fortunately, the subject of Greg/Ryan didn't come up again. *Un*fortunately, this meant I had to actually talk about some dumb trial.

"Don't forget to get your permission slip signed for our field trip this weekend!" Mr. Ikwang announces on our way out. "A trip to watch a real live mock trial competition at the high school!" Great. Just what I want to spend my weekend doing.

"Bye, guys," Bailey says. "I'll text you later." She says this last part to Luke. At least he has the decency to look uncomfortable.

"Mr. Ikwang," I say, approaching him. He's up at the front of the room, putting some stuff into a briefcase.

"Yes, Devon?"

"Can I have my phone back now? I really learned my lesson and I promise never to do it again." This is kind of true, but kind of not. I *have* learned my lesson, but more about not getting caught texting, not about not using my phone in school.

"It's still up in my classroom," he says. "Let me go grab it and I'll be right back."

"Thanks," I say gratefully. If I didn't have my phone, my mom would have definitely noticed. She's afraid I'm going to lose it, which is just completely ridiculous. I mean, how can I lose it when I'm constantly using it?

"So, are you going to call your mom and ask her about dinner?" I ask Luke.

"Yeah," he says. "I'm just going to go outside, since my cell doesn't get bars in here."

"I'll go with you," I say. We walk down the hall and step outside. I keep my eyes peeled, looking back into the school so that I don't miss Mr. Ikwang and my phone.

"Hey," Luke says to his mom when she answers. "I'm going to have dinner at Devon's, if that's okay." He covers the phone with his hand. "Can your parents give me a ride home after?"

"Sure," I say. I don't see why not. I mean, my mom invited him, the least she can do is provide transportation home. I peer through the door, looking for Mr. Ikwang. Where *is* he? His classroom is right at the top of the stairs. You'd think he'd be able to grab the phone and get down here by now.

"It's all set," Luke says, snapping his phone shut. "What are we having for dinner?"

"I'm not sure," I say. "But for your sake, you'd better hope it's takeout."

LAUREN BARNHOLDT

Luke laughs, looks around to make sure no one's watching, then leans over and brushes his lips against mine. I feel myself blush, the heat rising up to my cheeks.

"Here you go," Mr. Ikwang says brightly, opening the door and stepping outside. "Here's your phone, and I hope I won't have to see this anymore. Ever."

"You won't," I say. "Like I said, I've learned my lesson."

There's the sound of a horn honking, and I look up to see my mom's car in front of the school.

"Well, there's my mom!" I say. "See you later, Mr. Ikwang!"

Luke and I pile into the car, me in the front seat, and him in the back with Katie. I would have rather sat back there with him, but of course I couldn't really ask Katie to move, because it would have looked kind of weird to my mom.

"Why did that man have your phone?" Katie immediately wants to know. I turn around and give her a dirty look, but she doesn't get the message.

"Katie, be polite and say hello to Luke," my mom says. She pulls the minivan out of the circle in front of the school and onto the main road.

"Hello, Luke," Katie says. "And now for two questions. Number one, are you and Devon getting married, and number two, why did that mean man have Devon's phone?"

"What mean man?" I ask. I reach over and start fumbling with the CD player in my mom's car, hoping to find a good song that will distract Katie from both of her questions. Of course, she might start singing, but that's a risk I'm willing to take.

"That mean one, he was standing outside and he had a very mean look on his face."

"That was Mr. Ikwang," I say. "And he's not mean. He's really nice. Look, Katie, it's the Wiggles!" I figure having to listen to the annoying Wiggles is way better than Katie busting me for getting my phone taken away. Why is she here anyway? You'd think she could have stayed home with my dad. Of course, then it would have just been me, Luke, and my mom in the car, which probably would have been pretty uncomfortable.

"The Wiggles are for babies!" Katie screams. Wow. Okay, then. She turns to Luke. "I forgot your name." She sighs.

"I'm Luke, remember? We met when I came to your house a few weeks ago and we watched *The Cutting Edge*." A couple of weeks ago when I was babysitting Katie, and Luke and I were working on a school project, he came over and Katie made him watch some of this ice-skating movie, *The Cutting Edge*.

"Oh, right," Katie says. She sits back in her seat and pulls a book bag onto her lap from the floor of the car. "You're Devon's stupid boyfriend, and you got her in trouble when you came over, remember that, Devon?"

"Yes," I say, sighing. "I remember that." Something tells me this is not how Bailey Barelli's family treated Luke.

"So Luke," my mom says. "Devon says you two are in mock trial together?"

"Yes," he says. "Right now we're working our way through the Supreme Court cases."

"It's really interesting," I lie. In the backseat, Katie has pulled out a bag of crackers and is chewing on them noisily. I take a glance back there just in time to see one of the crumbs fly out of her mouth and land on Luke's sneaker. Ewww.

"Katie, um, I think you need a napkin," I try.

"I think you need to tell me why that mean-looking man had your phone, please."

"I told you, he's not mean, he's my teacher."

"Why did the teacher have your phone?" my mom asks, frowning.

"Um, he just . . ." I catch Luke's eye in the side

mirror. Crap. Now what? Do I make up something to tell my mom so that I don't get in trouble? I mean, is it *that* big of a deal to get caught texting in class? There are way worse things I could have done. Like cheat on a test for example. Or make out with Luke in the hallway, the way Lexi and Jared sometimes do. Of course, Lexi's mom wouldn't care about that, but my mom totally would. I'm just saying. And if I don't lie, if I just tell the truth, then Luke will see what a trustworthy person I am, right? Right?

"It wasn't a big deal," I say. "He just took my phone for the day because he caught me returning a text message in between classes. He wasn't even mad about it, they just have to do it because it's school rules." Not exactly the truth, but whatevs. I add a little eye roll to show that, you know, it's not a big deal. And that my mom shouldn't freak out. But then her hands tighten around the steering wheel, and I can tell it's going to be bad.

chapter nine

My mom's still upset when we pull into the driveway. I can tell she's trying to reign it all in since Luke is around and everything, but it's still a little uncomfortable.

"I just thought you and I had a promise to each other, that's all," she's saying. "That you wouldn't use the phone in school if we got you one."

"Um, well, I wasn't technically using it in school. I mean, yes, I was in school, but no, I wasn't in class, I told you, it was before the bell."

We're inside now, and Katie plops herself down on the floor of the foyer and holds her foot out to Luke.

"Untie my shoe, please, Luke," she says politely. Oh, geez. At least she remembered his name. And at least she's not wearing ballet slippers or something equally ridiculous. Luke hesitates for a second, then reaches down and starts untying her shoe.

The phone rings, and my sister rushes off to get it. She steps on Luke's foot as she goes, and my mom follows her into the kitchen.

"I'm sorry about all that," I say. "Katie's not usually so . . ." I'm trying to think of the word, and then I realize no matter *what* word I use, Katie usually *is* so. "Actually, she is."

"It's okay," he says, squeezing my hand. "They're your family. I'm looking forward to getting to know them."

Aww! How cute is Luke? Wanting to get to know my family even after my sister bossed him around, called him 'my stupid boyfriend' and then almost broke his toe when she stepped on it! And after my mom made an almost big deal about the texting. I mean, honestly. How embarrassing.

"Anyway," I say, "maybe we should go into the kitchen and look at some menus." My plan is to just nonchalantly open the drawer in the kitchen and pull out some menus, and then if my mom says anything, act like I just assumed we'd be ordering out. That way, maybe I can convince her. I considered telling her Luke had a bunch of weird food allergies, but then I realized it'd be hard to keep that going once Luke actually got here.

When we reach the kitchen, though, we find my mom at the stove, stirring something in a big pot. "Luke, I hope you like chicken and dumplings," my mom says. "It's been cooking all day."

"I love chicken and dumplings, thanks, Mrs. Delaney." Luke pulls out a chair and sits down at the table.

"Where's Dad?" I ask.

"He'll be home soon," my mom says. "He had to work late." My stomach rolls a little bit at this news. Working late? Isn't that the oldest excuse in the book for when parents are out, gallivanting around with other people?

"You can sit there," I say to Luke, pointing to the seat next to me. He'll be across from Katie, but hopefully she'll do a little better with the chicken and dumplings than she did with the crackers in the car.

"Devon, it's for you," Katie says, holding out the phone. "It's Greg."

Luke shoots me a look. My mom shoots me a look. Katie shoots me a look.

"Um, okay," I say. Why would Greg/Ryan be calling me? And why is he using his fake name?

"Hello?" I take the phone away from Katie and wonder if I can get away with pretending it's Mel.

"Hey, it's Ryan," Greg/Ryan says.

"Oh, hi." What I really want to say is, *Why are you calling me and how do you have my number and why have you picked the worst night to do so, the night my boyfriend is over for a supposedly relaxing family meal?* But all I say is, "Um, so what do you want?"

"I just wanted to touch base about this weekend. Now, I know I'm playing a juvenile delinquent, but do I need to dress like one, too?"

"Excuse me?"

"You know, like, does this person dress all hardcore, or is he just your normal, run-of-the-mill rich boy with a problem, like the ones that have dark secrets and are tortured?"

"I'm really not sure, I hadn't really thought that far ahead." Despite myself, I'm intrigued. Yes, Greg/Ryan's timing is completely off, but he brings up a good point. I don't think we can have him showing up at Mel's house wearing some kind of ripped clothes and carrying a switchblade. More likely he'd be a kid who comes from a good family, but maybe has a bad home life. Kind of like in this one movie I saw on Lifetime once, called, *A Stranger in the Family*. It was all about how the family didn't even know their own son once he started doing crazy things. "Hey, do you ever watch Lifetime?"

"No."

"Oh." So much for that. "Well, I think it's more like the rich kid thing."

"Good, that's what I was thinking, too. And I really think I can play this part well."

Hmmm. Does Greg/Ryan want to be an actor? I guess I could see that. Although he'd have to learn to listen to the director a little more, since he told Bailey Barelli that he still liked me, when he was specifically told not to. I want to ask him about this, but then I realize Luke is still in the kitchen with my mom, and neither one of them are talking. And it's not because they don't have anything to say to each other, but because they both want to hear what I'm saying.

"I have to go," I say, and hang up the phone before Greg/Ryan can respond. Please don't call back, please don't call back, I plead silently in my head.

"Who was that?" my mom asks.

"Oh, that was just Greg," I say. I slide into the seat next to Luke, praying my mom doesn't ask who Greg is.

"Who's—" But the phone rings, cutting her off. I almost jump out of my seat I'm so nervous.

"I'll get it!" I practically scream, running for the phone. Luke looks alarmed as I almost trip over Katie in my haste.

"Hello?" I say, breathless. I didn't even check the caller ID.

"Devon?" a male voice asks. But it's not Greg/Ryan. It's my dad.

"Oh, hi, Dad," I say, relieved. There's no way he'd be calling me if he were out with what's-her-face, the blonde from the Starbucks. Unless he's on his way home, and his guilt has gotten the best of him, and so he's calling to assuage those feelings. "Where are you?" I ask suspiciously.

"Listen, I'm not going to make dinner," he says. "There's some, uh, business I have to finish up at the office."

"Business, huh?"

"Yeah," he says. "Apologize to Luke for me, let him know I'll meet him next time. And tell your mom I should be home after I take care of this last thing."

"Sure," I say.

"Thanks, honey," he says. I hang up the phone.

"Who was that?" my mom asks.

"Dad," I say, slumping into the chair next to Luke. "He's not going to make it for dinner, he has to work late." I emphasize the words "work late" so that my mom can, you know, maybe get the hint that he's probably not *actually* working late. But she just starts opening up a tube of dough and dropping it into the chicken stew with a spoon.

Dinner passes by in a blur. I'm so upset that I can't even concentrate on what's being said. All I know is that my mom manages not to say anything too embarrassing (if you don't count how she tells Luke about how I used to have a blanket that I called Mr. Blankie when I was younger and if anyone tried to take it away from me I'd scream and cry), and Katie manages to chew with her mouth closed.

Luke is funny and cute and I can tell my mom likes him. After a dessert of ice cream sandwiches, when we're sitting around talking about the case we have to prepare for mock trial, my mom tells us that she and Katie will handle the dishes, and that we can go in the living room and work on our homework before she drives Luke home. I'm shocked. My mom, actually letting me go into the living room with Luke? Of course, the living room is right off the dining room, and there's no door connecting the two, but still.

"So," Luke says, once we've spread out all our books and papers. "Are you going to tell me what's got you so upset?"

"What do you mean?" I ask.

"Why you barely said one word during dinner?"

"I did say one word," I protest. "I yelled at my mom for telling that Mr. Blankie story."

Luke grins. "And you," I say, "better not tell anyone that story, not even Jared."

"Scout's honor," he says, crossing his heart.

"You're not a Boy Scout," I say. "Are you?"

"No."

"Then Scout's honor doesn't mean anything." I open my bag and pull out a pen, tapping it against my English binder thoughtfully. "You need to give me an honor on something you're actually a part of."

"Soccer player's honor?" he tries.

"Does the soccer team have some sort of unwritten code that you won't violate?" Somehow I doubt this, since all the soccer players I know throw spitballs at lunch and sometimes put gum in unsuspecting girls' hair.

"No," Luke admits. "But I think Scout's honor should be good enough, since you don't actually have to be a Scout to realize what a big undertaking that is."

"You're right," I say. My cell phone beeps, and I reach down into my bag and pull it out. FOUND THE PERFECT OUTFIT FOR CHALLENGING ROLE! it says. ALSO CAN MY FAKE NAME BE ETHAN? SOUNDS V. RICH! Ohmigod. How did Greg/Ryan get my cell phone number? Lexi, probably. I have to have a talk with her about violating others' privacy.

"Who's that?" Luke asks, as I quickly shove the phone back into my bag.

"Just Lexi," I say. "She wants to know about the dance."

There's a silence. "So," Luke says. "Are you going to tell me what's bothering you?"

"I told you, nothing." I open my English binder and run my finger over the first paper in there, an assignment sheet that lists our homework for the night, a response paper comparing and contrasting Romeo's cousin and his best friend as characters. Sigh.

"Is it about Greg?" Luke asks, shifting beside me on the couch. "Is that why you're upset?"

"What? No!"

"You got upset right after he called you, and you've been upset this whole time." He takes a deep breath. "What did he say to you? Do I need to kick his—"

"No!" My boyfriend wants to beat up a guy I've met

once in my life. I decide to take a deep breath and tell Luke about my dad. After all, Luke's parents are divorced, and maybe he'll have some insight. "It's my dad."

"Your dad? What about him?" Luke looks concerned, and I motion him a little closer to me so that my mom won't overhear us. He moves closer, until he's so close his leg is touching mine.

"I just . . ." I look down at my hands, take another deep breath, and then tell him the whole story. About how my dad acted weird on the phone that day. How Lexi and I saw him with that woman. And before I know it, I'm crying, fat little tears are sliding down my face and slipping off my cheeks and making wet spots on the sleeve of my shirt as I try to wipe them away.

"Hey, hey, hey," Luke says. He strokes my hair and pulls me into a hug. "You don't know what any of that means."

"I know," I say. "But let's be serious. I mean, he had to *work late*? And then he couldn't come home for dinner?"

"Yeah," he says slowly. He pulls away from the hug and looks at me, his eyes serious. "But Devon, no offense, you do tend to have kind of an overactive imagination."

"I do?"

"Yeah," he says. "Like how you thought something was going on between me and Bailey."

"I didn't think something was going on between you and Bailey," I say. And then, just to, you know, clear things up, I say, "Well, I didn't really *know* if something was going on with you and Bailey. I mean, you guys did used to go out, and there's all that texting and note-passing."

"Does the texting and note-passing really weird you out?" he says.

"I don't know," I say. "It's just . . . I don't know, it's complicated, all this ex-girlfriend stuff." I look down at my hands.

"Yeah, that's how I feel about Greg," he says. "I know he'll always be hard to compete with, since he was your first boyfriend."

"Yeah, but I don't see him ever. Or even talk to him." Luke raises his eyebrows, and I realize that Greg/Ryan just called me tonight. "Well, not that much anyway. You have to be with Bailey every single day at school, and after school, too, at mock trial."

"But I only want to be with you." And when he says it, something about the way his voice sounds makes me believe him.

"And I only want to be with you," I say.

"So it's a good thing we're together then." He smiles.

"A very good thing." I smile back at him, and he reaches out and takes my hand, drawing little circles on my palm with his finger.

"Devon?" he says. "I think you should talk to your dad. I'm sure it's probably nothing, but still. Just for your own peace of mind."

"You're right," I say. And I know he is. I just don't know if I'm ready to have that conversation.

chapter ten

"Of course I gave him your number, he kept asking for it," Lexi says. It's the next day after school, and she's standing in front of the mirror in her room, wearing a long, flowing, sheer lavender dress. It's scalloped on the top, with a sweetheart neckline. "No, no, no," Lexi declares. She pulls the dress off her head. "No good for the dance. I need something a little more me." She leaves the dress in a pile on the floor and goes skipping into her walk-in closet wearing nothing but her bra and underwear.

Neither me nor Mel (who's on the other side of the room, going through Lexi's bookshelves, looking for books she wants to borrow), are fazed by this display. We're used to it. Lexi dances around the gym locker room all the time like this. She just doesn't care.

"I thought you already had a dress for the dance," I say, flopping down on her bed and staring up at the ceiling.

"I *thought* I did, but I really need to keep my options open." She reappears holding a red, strapless short dress. She slides into it, and smiles at her reflection in the mirror. "Much better." She does a twirl, then looks at me. "Devi, did you get your dress yet?"

"No," I say. "I'm too depressed to think about the dance."

"Stop acting like a drama queen," Lexi instructs. She twirls in front of the mirror, the dress swishing all around her.

"Yeah," Mel says. She holds up a book. "I'm taking this one, too, is that okay?"

"Sure," Lexi says, waving her hand. "Take whatever you want."

"I'm not being dramatic," I say. "My dad is having an affair, hello! That is a huge deal."

"Just because you saw him with some woman in Starbucks?" Mel asks. "No offense, Devon, but you do kind of have an overactive imagination."

"You forgot about the weird phone call and the *working late.*" What is up with everyone telling me I have an overactive imagination? It's not *that* bad. I mean, yeah, I have created some secret lives for myself. And one time last year when this woman asked me to watch her computer while she ran to the bathroom at the library, I did get all nervous thinking maybe she was some kind of spy and the computer was a bomb. But seeing your dad with another woman? That is pretty much something that you cannot misinterpret.

"Hey," I say to Lexi, suddenly remembering. "Where were you in mock trial yesterday?"

A look of guilt passes over Lexi's face, and she and Mel exchange a look. "What?" I ask. "What's going on with you two?"

"Um, well," Lexi says. She turns away from the mirror and twists her hands nervously. Suddenly Mel gets very busy arranging all the books she's going to be borrowing into a pile. "The thing is, mock trial isn't really for me."

"You're quitting? But Lexi, you should have an extracurricular." I don't really mean that. About the extracurricular thing. Yeah, she should have one, I guess, but I don't really care if she does. What I do care about is her staying in mock trial with me, so I'm not left alone with Bailey and Kim.

"I do," she says.

"You do what?" I'm confused.

"I do have an extracurricular." Her eyes flash to Mel, who's still busy arranging. And not looking at me. Lexi clears her throat, and then says finally, "I joined radio."

"You *what?*"

"I joined radio," she says. She walks over to her dresser, where she pulls out a pair of red patterned tights and pulls them on. Then she takes a pair of shoes off the shoe rack over the back of her closet door and slides into them. "Oh, Devi, please don't be mad. I just couldn't take another day of Mr. Ikwang going on and on about the Constitution and juries."

She couldn't take another day? She was only in mock trial for one day. Sigh. Although I know what she means. I don't like mock trial, and my experience with things that you don't like right away is that they don't usually get better.

"I'm not mad," I say.

"You can still join, you know," Mel says. She abandons the books and comes to sit next to me on the bed. "There's still room in radio."

"Ooh, yes, Devi, you totally have to! We're going to do a school advice show, and it's going to be airing in the mornings and maybe even during lunch." She pulls a skirt out of her closet and throws it on the floor. "Ugh, what is *that* doing in there?"

"You're getting rid of this?" Mel asks, picking it up. It's long and pale green, with a silver overlay and beading.

"It's like three seasons ago," Lexi says. "You can have it if you want."

"I wouldn't have anywhere to wear it," Mel says, running her fingers over the beads.

"Um, hello? The dance," I remind her.

"Not going," Mel says.

"You're not going to ask Dylan?" I ask. Not that I'm surprised. I figured she wouldn't. It's just not her style.

"What?!" Lexi yells. "Mel, this is ridiculous." She turns to me. "You should see them in radio. They are soo cute together."

"They are?"

"Yeah, like he's always asking her advice, and he's always coming up with dumb excuses to talk to her, like asking her for paper and stuff. That's totally what Jared used to do with me before he asked me out."

A lump rises up in my throat. I'm sad Lexi's the

one who gets to see Mel interact with Dylan. I'm not jealous of them being friends. In fact, I *want* them to be friends, since Mel was my best friend since forever, and Lexi was my friend this summer, and I love the fact that they actually get along now even though they're so different. But I'm sad that I'm not getting to see this part of Mel's life. And then I think about how if she goes away to private school, I'm not going to be able to see *any* part of her life, and I start to feel even sadder.

I mean, here I am, wasting valuable Mel time with mock trial! I throw myself across the bed and feel sorry for myself.

"Call him," Lexi demands. She picks Mel's cell up off the bed and hands it to her. "Now."

"She can't just call him," I say, worried in spite of myself. "She doesn't have his number."

"Yes, she does," Lexi says, her eyes gleaming. "He gave it to her yesterday. He said it was for when they need to start talking about programming the station, but that was totally just an excuse." She rolls her eyes, then disappears back into her closet. "What do we think about stripes with prints?" she asks, appearing with a weird-looking dress.

"No," I say.

"I'm going to do it!" Mel says suddenly. Lexi and I look at her, shocked.

"You are?"

"Yes!" she declares. "I'm going to do it." She reaches over, picks up her cell phone, and scrolls through until she finds his number. She pushes the green button before she can stop herself. Ohmigod, ohmigod, ohmigod.

"Are you sure about this?" I ask. Mel looks a little pale, like she might throw up.

"Too late now," Lexi says cheerfully. "She's already dialed. If she hangs up, he'll know she's pranking him."

"Maybe he won't answer," I offer to Mel hopefully. But it doesn't do anything to help the sick look on her face, and she reaches out and grabs my hand. Ow. Mel's got a killer grip. I can hear the ringing through her phone. One ring, two rings, three rings . . . just when I'm certain it's about to go to voice mail, a male voice answers. A very deep male voice. Wow. Mel's *definitely* going after an eighth grader.

"Hello?" the deep male voice says.

"Hello?" Mel squeaks. Her grip on my hand tightens.

"Ow!" I say.

"Hello?" the voice says again. Mel's silent. She's moving her mouth but nothing's coming out. It's like something you'd see in a movie, and you'd go, *Oh, that would never happen in real life, that girl is freaking out over nothing*, but it *is* happening in real life, right here in Lexi's bedroom.

I reach over and give Mel a pinch on her shoulder. But she still can't talk.

"Uh, hello," I say, leaning over and speaking into the phone. "It's me, Mel." Mel's eyes grow large, and Lexi stifles a giggle. Ohmigod. Now I am pretending to be Mel. He's definitely going to know. I mean, we sound nothing alike. Do we? What does Mel's voice sound like? Softer than mine. Kind of . . . breathy.

"Oh, hey, Mel," Dylan says. "What's up?"

"Not much," I say, trying to sound quiet and breathy.

"Are you okay?" he asks, sounding confused. "Are you wheezing?"

"Uh, no," I say, ditching the breathy and resorting to just sounding a little soft. "I think I'm getting a cold."

"That sucks," he says. "I think something's going around."

"Yeah." I look at Mel, but she's still frozen. And now I'm talking to her crush about being sick, which is definitely not how the conversation was supposed to go. I mean, who wants to be equated with germs and runny roses? "Um, anyway, I was calling to ask you a question."

Mel looks over at me, and nods.

"Um, well, I wanted to know—"

But before I can get the question out, Mel somehow gets a hold of herself and breaks in. "I was wondering if you'd like to go to the dance with me this weekend."

There's a pause where it seems like everything stops. And even though it can't be more than a second, I think it's the anticipation of waiting for Dylan's response coupled with the surprise that Mel took over the phone call that makes it seem like it's years. And then, finally, through the phone, I hear him say, "I'd love to."

"Okay," Mel says. "Cool. So, um, I'll see you in school tomorrow and we can make plans then, okay, thanks, bye!" She hangs up the phone and looks at me in shock. Okay, not the smoothest way to end the call, but still. Much better than pranking and/or freezing up.

There's a moment of silence, and then we all start screaming.

When I get home from Lexi's, my dad's in the kitchen, whistling and making a pot of chili at the stove.

"What's this?" I ask.

"Turkey chili," he says cheerfully. He holds the spoon out and I take some. It's warm and a little spicy, just the way I like it.

"Delish," I say. "But, um, why isn't Mom cooking?"

"Do I really have to answer that question?" he asks. He says it like it's funny, and under normal circumstances, it would be, but not when you're having an affair. You shouldn't make fun of your wife's cooking then. It's like rubbing salt in the wound. Of course, my dad doesn't know that I know about him and his little mystery woman, but still.

"So, Dad," I say, trying to sound nonchalant. "You had to work late the other day, huh?"

"Yeah," he says, adding a little more chili powder to the chili.

"What were you working on so late?" I ask. I get up and wander toward the refrigerator to pour myself a glass of lemonade. But I'm watching him out of the corner of my eye, and I don't think it's my imagination that a look of guilt passes across his face. Aha!

"Just work stuff," he says. "Boring, actually." He

wipes his hand on the kitchen towel that's slung over his shoulder.

"I like boring." I sit back down at the table and take a long sip of my drink. "In fact, I was thinking about having you come in for career day, and I'd like to hear more about what you do."

"You would, huh?" he says. He sounds like maybe he doesn't believe me. Good. I hope he knows I'm on to him. I hope he knows that maybe just maybe I saw him at the coffee shop that day, and that there's no way I'm letting him get away with this. He pulls a chair out across the table from me and sits down. "I think I know what this has to do with."

"You do?" He does?

"Yes." He looks at me. Oh, God. My dad is about to confess that he's having an affair. "You're upset because I wasn't here to meet Luke."

"Oh." Pfffttt. I feel like a balloon that's just had all its air let out. "No. I mean, yeah, I wish you could have met him, but you'll meet him another time I'm sure."

Honestly, it probably would have been weirder if my dad were here when Luke came to dinner. First, because he probably would have tried to get all fatherly on me and ask Luke a bazillion questions. And second, because I wouldn't have been able to tell Luke about what was going on with my dad. And it felt nice to let that out.

"I will definitely meet him another time." He pats my shoulder and then returns to the stove. "Maybe on the night of the dance. Your mother has a whole thing planned, with pictures, the works."

"She does?" Wow. It didn't take long for my mom to get on board the dance train. Although I doubt she's going to let me pre- and post-party at Lexi's. I wonder if she's on board the new dress train, too.

"Anyway," my dad says, turning down the stove. "I'm gonna just let this simmer for a bit, and it'll be ready for when I get back around dinnertime."

"Where are you going?" I ask suspiciously.

"The gym," my dad says, and my stomach drops to my shoes.

I call Luke because I don't know what else to do.

"Hey," he says when he answers. "I was just thinking about you."

"My dad's at the gym," I blurt.

"O-kaay." He sounds confused.

"I was at Lexi's, and we printed out this list and it said that the gym is a VERY BAD SIGN."

"Devon," Luke says. "You're not making any sense."

"Keep it down in there!" Katie calls from the living room. "*Hardball with Chris Matthews* is starting on MSNBC!"

Actually, I *should* probably keep it down. Don't want my mom or Katie overhearing me.

"Okay," I say, whispering. "I was at Lexi's earlier, right? Just trying on clothes and Mel asked Dylan to the dance, and then we went on her computer."

"What?" Luke says. "I can't hear you."

"I was at Lexi's." I try to raise my voice a little bit, and stretch the phone as far as it will go into the kitchen, away from Katie. Why oh why do we not have a cordless phone in here? Better yet, why am I not on my cell phone? I consider switching over, but then decide it would be too much effort to go and call Luke back, so I just cover the mouthpiece with my hand and hope for the best.

"You were at Lexi's," he says. "Okay, and . . ."

"And we looked up stuff online about the signs of affairs. You know, like how to tell if your husband is having one." I don't tell him the part about how I was trying to apply them to our own relationship, and figure out if I should be worried about him and Bailey. This information is being given on a need-to-know basis.

"Oh, Devon," he says, sighing. "Why would you do that?"

"Um, because I wanted to know if my dad was having an affair?" Isn't it obvious? Luke's usually much smarter about this stuff.

"Devon, the way to find out what's going on with your dad isn't by looking up stuff on the internet."

"But the internet is the information superhighway," I tell him.

"Yes, but that superhighway is also filled with tons of people writing tons of things that make no sense. Anyone can post whatever they want."

"Oh, well, I know that." I've stretched the phone cord all the way over to the other side of the room now, and I grab a cushion off one of our kitchen chairs and plop it on the floor. Then plop myself down on top of it. "That's why I made sure that the article was written by someone with a PhD. And it said that one of the signs is working late, and taking more of an interest in one's appearance, aka, going to the gym, buying new clothes, etc."

"And because your dad is going to the gym, and you read it in some article, you think that it's true?"

"Yes."

"Devon, that's crazy."

"It's not crazy."

"Yes, it is."

"No, it isn't."

"Yes, it is."

Are we really fighting about this?

"Look, you need to ask your dad about it."

"Yeah," I say. I feel the tears burning up behind my eyes. "Listen, I gotta go. But I'll call you later, okay?"

And I hang up before he tries to convince me not to.

chapter eleven

Stephanie. Her name is Stephanie. The woman my dad was meeting that day. I know because after he left for the gym, I looked at his phone. I know, that was very bad and a very big violation of his privacy. But I couldn't help it. It was just sitting there, on the counter, plugged into the charger. It was almost screaming, *Devon, come and look at me, please!* So I just very carefully maybe kind of sort of went over and peeked at it. And then I maybe kind of sort of just went over and scrolled through his call log.

I mean, come on! My dad hasn't been to the gym in, like, forever. I never even heard of him wanting to go jogging or anything. And now all of a sudden he's all about getting in shape? So now I'm sitting in the kitchen, with the chili on the stove, wondering what I should do next. Tell my mom? I don't exactly want to be the bearer of *that* bad news. Plus, what if my imagination *is* going all crazy? I'll get everyone all worked up over nothing.

Maybe Stephanie is just a friend. Or maybe she's his boss or something.

Maybe if I could talk to this ridiculous Stephanie person, I'd know. Like, for example, if I just happened to go over to his phone and maybe dial her number, and I got a voice mail that was like, "Hi, you've reached the voice mail of Stephanie, boss of the company" or something. Then I would definitely know it was just a co-worker.

I pick up my dad's phone and run my fingers over the buttons. I can hear Katie in the other room, talking to the television set. ("That is not an Olympic scandal! That is just a misunderstanding!") And my mom is running the vacuum upstairs. No one would need to know. I could just call, and hang up. She's probably used to hang ups. Aren't people who are having affairs always hanging up on each other?

I scroll through the names until I get to "Stephanie."

I know it's definitely going too far, even for me, but I can't help it. I push the call button before I can change my mind. One ring . . . two . . . three . . . Please, please, please let it be a work friend, I say a silent chant in my head.

The sound of the vacuum disappears, which means my mom is done vacuuming. Not good. What if she comes down here and sees me with my dad's phone to my ear? What if she's all, "Devon, hand over that phone," and then she takes it and is like, "Why are you calling a woman named Stephanie" and then I have to confess everything to her? What if—

"Hello?" a woman's voice says on the other end. And I just know it's her. She sounds blond. And very sort of throaty, like she has a cold. Or is a smoker. I hope my dad doesn't plan on marrying her and moving us all into a smoker's house. I have very sensitive lungs.

"John? I was hoping you'd call, listen, are you able to get away for an hour or so? I have something I'm just dying to show you."

Well. That settles that. I switch the phone back off. Then I go up to my room, lie down on my bed, and burst into tears.

Bzzzz. Bzzzz. What? *Bzzzz.* I'm half asleep, in bed, and my phone is vibrating on my nightstand, making a horrible buzzing sound that sounds loud enough to wake up the whole house. But is, of course, only waking up me.

I check the display. Five new text messages.

Number one:

YOU SHOULD SEE MY OUTFIT FOR MY NEXT ROLE, BABE! From: Greg/Ryan

Number two:

DO YOU WANT TO GO SHOPPING FOR DRESSES AFTER MEL'S TMR? From: Lexi

Number three:

ANSWER UR PHONE!! I CAN'T BELIEVE I ASKED HIM! From: Mel

Number four:

WHAT TIME SHOULD I BE THERE TOMORROW? from Greg/Ryan

Number five:

HEY—YOU NEVER CALLED ME BACK. MISS U, SEE YOU IN SCHOOL. From: Luke.

I check the clock next to my bed. Seven a.m. Ugh. I must have fallen asleep, and no one bothered to wake me up—they just let me sleep through the night. Not that I would have been much company, I mean, I am not talking to my dad, and I wouldn't even know how to act around my mom.

I take a quick shower, tie my hair back, and slip into jeans and a soft pink wool sweater. When I get to school, Luke's waiting for me at my locker.

"Hey," he says. He goes to hug me, and I return it halfheartedly. "What's wrong?"

"Nothing's wrong," I say. "Except for the fact that my dad is having an affair." I spin the dial on my combination lock, and I'm so upset, that I go past the right number and have to start over twice.

"Are you still on that?" Luke ask, smiling at me like I'm a child who's just said something cute. "Really, Devon."

"Is that all you have to say, is 'really, Devon'? How would you like to know that it really *is* true? You probably wouldn't feel so happy then, would you?"

Luke takes a step back, like I slapped him. "Hey," he says. "I was just trying to help, you don't have to go crazy."

"Crazy? I'm being *crazy*?" I'm yelling a little bit now, and Luke leans in close.

"Calm down," he says. "Listen, maybe we should talk about this later."

"No thanks," I say. "I don't really want to talk about it at all."

And then I slam my locker door shut and stomp off down the hall.

Okay. So maybe that was a little dramatic. I mean, Luke *was* just trying to help. And there's no way he could have known that I looked in my dad's phone and called some woman back who said something very *affair-like* to me, thinking it was my dad. But God, it's like, you make up one fake boyfriend, and everyone thinks you have an overactive imagination, and you can never get taken seriously again. And yeah, okay, so maybe I made up *two* fake boyfriends, but Luke doesn't know that. He just knows about the one fake boyfriend from a few weeks ago. And when it comes to parents potentially having affairs, one should get the benefit of the doubt.

"Well, you shouldn't have ignored him at lunch, Devi, that wasn't very nice." Lexi admonishes. She's sitting at Mel's kitchen table, while we wait for Greg/ Ryan to get here.

"I wasn't *ignoring* him," I say. "He wasn't talking to me." All throughout lunch, things with Luke and I were definitely awkward. He hardly even looked at me, and all we said to each other were a few words about the weekend. Oh, and at one point, he told me I had mustard on my hand. I was eating one of those soft pretzels, and I can never keep the mustard from getting all over.

"You could tell he was upset," Mel says. She's sitting next to me, munching on sour cream and onion chips and looking surprisingly calm for someone who's academic future is maybe about to be decided.

"You could?" I perk up.

"Yes," Mel reports. "I saw him looking over at you with a very sad look on his face a bunch of times."

"Is that true, Lexi?" I ask. No answer. "Lexi?" I give her ankle a little kick under the table.

"Oh, sorry," she finally says. "I was thinking about how sometimes when I wear purple, it washes me out, even though it's my fave color. So unfair." She sighs. "Anyway, what was the question?"

"Did Luke look sad at lunch today?"

"Oh, yes, very sad, kind of like a puppy dog."

"Well, he didn't seem too sad to me, talking to Bailey the whole time." Luke and Bailey got involved in some dumb conversation about some case they want to ask Mr. Ikwang if they can do in mock trial. And I couldn't follow it, because it wasn't a case I'd ever heard of, it was something they just heard about or knew about somehow. And they kept going on and on, and I'm not sure if it was my (overactive?) imagination or not, but I could swear Bailey was throwing me little smirks.

"Oh, come on, Devon," Mel says. "He can't just ignore her when she's talking to him. Luke's a nice guy, he would never do that. And would you really want to be with someone who did?"

"I guess not," I grumble. My cell phone beeps then, and I look down. A text from Luke! "Sry about this morning," it says. "Do U want to come over and talk? ☺" Yay! Luke wants to talk it out! I mean, he wouldn't have said he was sorry if he didn't, right? And he sent a smiley! A smiley definitely means he wants to work it out. I'll go over there, and his mom will make us hot chocolate (not sure why I think that, since she's never made us hot chocolate before, but it sounds nice), and then we'll talk for hours and hours, and we'll make up, and he'll tell me that Bailey is the most ridiculous, horrible, insane—

Crap. I can't go over there. I have to be here for Mel. I can't just abandon her and Lexi before Greg/ Ryan gets here. But what can I tell Luke? If I say I'm hanging out with Lexi and Mel, he'll think I don't want to come over that badly. But I can't tell him it's because

Greg/Ryan is coming over to pretend to be Ethan.

"I'm sry 2," I text back. "Can't come over now, at my grams—will cal u later xxxo"

The text is just going through when the doorbell rings.

"He's here," Mel says, her face drained of color. She puts down the bag of chips.

"Yup," Lexi says happily. She claps her hands.

The plan is pretty simple. Basically, we told Mel's mom that Lexi's cousin might stop by. Then when he gets here, we're going to let her know he goes to St. Mary's. Then hopefully Greg/Ryan will say tons of weird stuff as Ethan so that Mel's mom will realize private school isn't full of all the great influences she thinks it is.

I take a sour cream and onion chip out of the bag and wonder if Greg/Ryan will be any good at playing a bad boy. I mean, how hard was it to play my boyfriend? All he had to do was play himself, pretty much. And he even kind of screwed that up. Hopefully we won't be in the same situation here.

"Oh, hello," I can hear Mel's mom saying from the living room. "You must be Lexi's cousin."

"Yes," Greg/Ryan says. "I'm Corbin." Corbin? Who said anything about a Corbin?

"I thought his name was supposed to be Ethan," Mel whispers.

I shrug. I thought his name was supposed to be Ethan, too. But now that I think about it, Corbin definitely sounds much better. Kind of uppity, in a good way. I mean, you could find an Ethan at any public school in America, I bet. There's a bunch of them at my school, even. But a Corbin? A Corbin you definitely have to go to a private school to find.

"It's a pleasure to meet you," I hear Greg/Ryan saying. "What a lovely home you have."

"Why, thank you, Corbin," Mel's mom says. Their voices are getting closer to the kitchen, and when they finally appear, I do a double take. Greg/Ryan is wearing a suit! Well, not all of a suit. Just the top part. The jacket. Over a shirt and tie, with a pair of jeans. He looks . . . kind of cool. But in a hipsterish sort of way, like he doesn't really care if people think he's nerdy.

"I assume you all will be working in the kitchen?" Mel's mom asks. You can tell she totally doesn't want us alone in Mel's room with a boy. Which doesn't make much sense, since I have a boyfriend, Corbin's supposedly Lexi's cousin, and Mel likes someone else. But parents don't think that way.

"Of course," Mel says.

"Charmed," Greg/Ryan says to Mel's mom.

And then he does something totally unexpected. He takes her hand and kisses it! Mel's mom's hand! Right there in the kitchen! And she gets totally flustered and is all, "Charmed as well, Corbin." But you can tell she kind of likes it. Parents always like that stuff. They think it's old-fashioned.

"Wow," I say, once Mel's mom is in the other room and safely out of earshot. "What was up with that?"'

"What do you mean?" Greg/Ryan asks. He looks confused as he plops down into the chair next to me. "Hey, babe," he says. "Nice to see you again." I guess when Greg/Ryan is playing Corbin, he still calls people "babe."

"She means kissing my mom's hand," Mel says. "You're not supposed to be all nice to her. The point is to get her to hate you, remember?"

"That shouldn't be hard," Lexi says. She gets up from the kitchen table and opens Mel's fridge, scanning the contents.

"I have to ease into it," Greg/Ryan says. "I can't just come in here acting all crazy"—he moves his hands around and makes a weird face—"from the get-go."

"Why not?" I ask. This theory doesn't make much sense. He should definitely be crazy from the get-go.

Once you give someone a chance to like you, they can make up all sorts of excuses for your behavior.

"Can I have this yogurt?" Lexi asks from the fridge, holding up a blue container.

"Because," Ryan/Greg says, "we have to make it *believable*. We want her to think that from the outside, I look like a great guy. But that when you get down to it, I'm trouble." He drums his fingers on the table. Greg/Ryan has very nice nails. I wonder if that's something he did special just to play Corbin, or if he always keeps them so nice.

"I guess so," I say uncertainly. "But we don't have that much time."

"Do you trust me?" Greg/Ryan asks. Mel and I look at each other warily, and I can tell we're both thinking the same thing: And that's *not really*. But we don't have much of a choice.

"They don't trust you at all," Lexi says. "And I don't blame them." She holds up the yogurt container and shakes it a little. "Yogurt, hello?"

"Yes, you can have the yogurt," Mel says. Lexi smiles, grabs a spoon out of the drawer, and throws the peel-back top of the yogurt into the garbage.

"We need to get your mom back in here," I say. "Let's ask her if we can order a pizza."

"Good idea, babe," Greg/Ryan says.

"Can you not call me babe?" I ask.

"Ooh, feminist, eh?" He leans back in his chair and smiles. "I get it." Sigh.

"Mooo—om," Mel calls. "Can you come here for a second?"

Mel's mom returns to the kitchen. "Oh," she says when she sees Lexi with the yogurt. "I see you've found my special organic wheat germ yogurt that costs three dollars a container."

"Wheat germ?" Lexi frowns. "I was wondering why it tasted so grainy." She wrinkles her small nose and drops the rest of the yogurt into the garbage.

"Mom, can we order pizza?" Mel asks. "We're hungry."

"Sure," Mel's mom says. "Grab the menus from the drawer."

"I'll do it," Greg/Ryan says, jumping up and heading over to the menu drawer.

"Why, thank you, Corbin," Mel's mom says. It takes me a second to figure out who she's talking to. I've already forgotten that we're supposed to be calling Greg/Ryan Corbin. I think of him as Greg/Ryan. Or possibly Ethan. He should be like one of those bands that just goes by a symbol. Much less confusing that way.

"No problem," Greg/Ryan says, leafing through the menus. "I'm happy to be of help when your girl has the day off."

"My girl?" Mel's mom looks confused. I'm confused, too. Is he talking about Mel? Mel's the only girl in her family. And she's sitting right at the table. Is he trying to talk in some kind of weird rich people talk?

"Yeah, you know, your housekeeper, your maid, your hired help." He looks around. "She must have the day off. I can tell because we're ordering our own pizza. And well, because—" he wrinkles his nose and trails off as he surveys the mess of chips and sodas that are sitting on the table.

Gasp! Is he calling Mel's house dirty? She def won't like that. Mel's mom is a total neat freak. She makes Mel separate all her shirts into colors before hanging them in her closet. And she alphabetizes all their DVDs and even the shows that come up on their Tivo.

"Oh," Greg/Ryan's face falls. "Where are the gourmet pizza menus? I can't really have anything but goat cheese, regular dairy just doesn't sit well with my complexion." He draws out the word goat, and says it like "gooooatt."

"I hate goat cheese," Lexi says, wrinkling her nose

some more. She's obviously forgotten that Greg/Ryan is just playing a role.

"I don't like goat cheese either," Mel says, taking the menus from Greg/Ryan. "I want to order from Pizza Palace."

"Ooh, Pizza Palace." I imagine their big sheet pizza, oozing with extra cheese and pepperoni, and my stomach grumbles. "That sounds good. Uh, is that okay with you, Ethan?"

"You mean Corbin," Mel says, a panicked look crossing her eyes.

"Right," I say. "Sorry, Corbin, I forgot your name for a second."

But Mel's mom didn't notice the slip-up at all, since she's watching as Greg/Ryan very carefully removes his sport coat, looks around for someone to take it, and then, seeing no one's going to, lays it on the back of his chair. I notice his nails again as he does it. Greg/Ryan definitely might have gotten a manicure before all of this. He's really getting into it.

"I'll order the food," Greg/Ryan says. He takes his cell phone out of his pocket and checks the screen. "Oh, great," he says. Then he does this big huge sigh, like he can't believe what horrible news he's just gotten.

"What?" I ask eagerly. "What is it?" This is sort of

like a show for me, too, since I have no idea what Greg/
Ryan has up his sleeve. It's kind of fun, like watching a
play or something. It *almost* makes up for the fact that
he's caused so many problems in my relationship with
Luke. And, of course, it helps that this is the last time
I'm ever going to see him. I'm feeling very forgiving
because of that.

"I just got a very important text," Greg/Ryan says.
"Excuse me." He walks into the dining room and we
can see him talking quietly into his phone.

"He's kind of an odd character, your cousin," Mel's
mom says to Lexi. She has a confused look on her face.

Lexi shrugs. "He never used to be like that. I think
it's because all his friends at St. Mary's are rich and
very sheltered." For a second I worry Lexi may have
gone too far, but then she just goes back to looking
through Mel's cupboards. She pulls down a box of
crackers. "Do you mind if I have some of these?" she
asks. "To tide me over until the pizza comes?"

"No," Lexi's mom says. "Uh, so he goes to St.
Mary's, does he?"

"Yeah." Lexi reaches into the box of crackers and
pulls one out, then takes a big crunching bite. "He's
gone there for the past two years."

"Well, what does—"

Suddenly, from the dining room comes the sound of Greg/Ryan yelling. "No! I said by Monday and I meant by Monday! Well, figure it out! How hard can it be? Make! It! Work!" There's a pause, and then his voice gets softer. "Good, that's better. See how easy it is to do business with me?"

Yikes. "Does Greg/Ryan have his own business?" I whisper to Lexi.

"I have no idea," she whispers back.

"Sorry about that rudeness on my part," Greg/Ryan says, returning to the kitchen and sliding his phone back into his bag. I do a double take. I hadn't realized it before, but Greg/Ryan doesn't have a normal book bag. He's carrying a murse! A leather man purse with a big thick strap and lots of buckles! Wow. I wonder where he got that.

"Do you have your own business?" I ask. I can hardly wait for the answer.

"Yes," he says. "Actually, I do." He reaches over and picks up the menu for Pizza Palace off the table. "Now, where was I?"

"What's your business?" I press.

"I do your standard homework running," he says. "With a fifteen percent commission off the top. Of course, in this economy, business has been slow, and it doesn't help when you get employees that want to take the weekend off to party." He scans the menu. "I tell them, 'look, if you want to be a slacker, be a slacker, if you want to be successful, then be successful.' I don't really have time to mess around with laziness."

Mel's mom's mouth is wide open. Lexi, Mel, and I are wrapped around Greg/Ryan's every word. It's definitely like some kind of movie, and he's the star.

"What's homework running?" Mel's mom asks. Her tone sounds wary, like she almost doesn't want to know.

"You know, getting people's homework and papers done for them." Greg/Ryan pushes his hair out of his face. I notice a very expensive looking watch that slides down his wrist as he does it. "I make a list of things that need to be done for people, name a price, and then farm them out to the kids that work for me. They get paid for doing the homework, the customer gets a great assignment, I take fifteen percent, and everyone's happy."

Mel's mom is now openly gaping. I can tell what she's thinking. Not only is that a horrible business to be running, but he's being so cavalier about it. Like, he's just telling her about it, sitting right here at Mel's table, almost bragging to her. And she's a parent.

"Isn't that against the rules at St. Mary's?" Mel's mom asks, trying to keep her voice even.

"Of course," Greg/Ryan says. "But the administration can't really do anything. My parents give so much money to that school, it's easier for them to look the other way. Plus, with all the scholarship kids doing the homework for the other kids, everyone has a higher GPA." He smiles. "Which looks great in the school brochures. That's probably one of the reasons you wanted Mel to go there, right?" He grins. Mel's mom just stares at him, and me, Lexi, and Mel are just watching, hanging on every word.

"Excuse me," Mel's mom finally says. "I think I'm going to go and watch television in the other room. You kids go ahead and order the pizza."

"That," I say, looking at Greg/Ryan with new respect, "was awesome." And then I give him a high five.

chapter twelve

We're so happy about how things went with Greg/Ryan, that we all decide to go to the mall. Well, Mel, Lexi, and I decide to go to the mall, and Greg/Ryan has to come along, too, since his mom isn't picking him up until later. I still need to get something to wear to the semi-formal, and Lexi and Greg/Ryan want to play DDR. So when we get there, Mel heads with me to help me find a dress, and Lexi and Greg/Ryan take off for the arcade.

"What do you think of this?" I ask Mel, stepping out of the stall and into the communal area of the dressing room. I'm wearing a long, puffy green dress with emeralds all up and down the side.

"Um, it's a little bit much for a middle school dance," Mel says, frowning.

"You're right," I say. I head back into the dressing room.

"Do you need anything else?" a voice calls from outside. The salesgirl. A very annoying one, fyi. As soon as we walked into the store, she pounced on us like a cat on its toy. Which is how I ended up with this green dress. She kept insisting that green was my color. Not sure why or how she decided this, since I don't really wear much green. Also, how can green really be anyone's color? I guess if you have red hair. Red hair is very conducive to wearing green, I think. Maybe green really is my color, and if I'd been wearing it all along, Luke wouldn't have been texting and passing notes with Bailey Barelli in English.

"No, she's fine," Mel says. "But we'll let you know."

"Okay, but we just got in—"

"No, really," Mel says. "WE'RE FINE."

I hear the salesgirl's feet moving away from the dressing room. "Thanks," I say. I didn't realize Mel could be so assertive. I guess once you ask your crush out to the dance, dealing with a salesgirl is nothing.

I'm trying to unbutton the green dress (it has this weird setup where you need to unbutton it all the way down your side, and then a side zipper starts at the waist), but it's not going so well.

"Have you figured out what you're going to do about your dad yet?" Mel calls from the other side of the door. I filled her in on the latest while we were wandering around the store, picking out dresses for me to try on.

"No," I say. "For right now I'm just avoiding him." What is wrong with this zipper? The dress isn't tight or anything, but I think I somehow managed to snag the zipper. But on what? I give it another tug.

"Oh, good plan," Mel says. "When in doubt, avoid, avoid, avoid."

"Exactly," I say, nodding even though I don't know if I really agree with this theory. I give the dress zipper another tug, but it still doesn't move. "Um, Mel?" I venture. "I think I'm stuck."

"Is the door locked?" she asks, jiggling the handle. "Let me go and get that salesgirl."

"No!" I say. "Um, it's not the door. It's the dress." I open the door and Mel slides in. "I'm stuck in it."

"Oh," Mel says. She grabs the zipper and tries to

tug it, but it doesn't budge. "What is it stuck on?"

"Nothing that I can see," I tell her. "But it *must* be stuck on something."

"I don't think so," Mel says.

"They're right back here," we hear the salesgirl saying from outside the dressing room. "At least, they were." There's a knock on the door.

"Yes?" I say, trying to sound haughty like I've heard Lexi do when she gets annoyed with the salespeople.

"Is everything all right in there, miss?"

"Yes," I say. "Everything is just fine." I hope they don't have to cut me out of this thing. My mom would be super mad if I had to buy a dress that had to be cut off of me.

"Well, your friends are here," she says. "And why are there two of you in one fitting room?" She sounds like having two people in one fitting room is the same sort of offense as making a nuclear weapon or something.

"I'll take over from here, Susie." Lexi's voice comes floating over the dressing room door. She knocks on the door.

"Yes, well—" Susie starts, but Lexi cuts her off.

"Honestly, I said we have it. Now if you want your commission, go!"

I hear the sound of Susie's feet as she shuffles away.

"Um, I don't think I'm supposed to be back here," I hear Greg/Ryan say. Duh. He's definitely right. He shouldn't be back in the girls changing room area. There's a bench right outside for husbands and boy-friends to sit on. Greg/Ryan is definitely not my boy-friend, but still. He could just go sit on the bench. It's totally allowed for fake ex-boyfriends, I'm sure.

"Lexi," I hiss. "I'm stuck. And I need help."

"You're what?" Lexi asks, banging on the door. "Why is Mel in there with you? Come out for God's sakes!"

I push open the door to the dressing room. "I'm stuck," I say, holding up my hands. "The dress won't come off me."

"Come out here," Lexi says. "And we'll get help, I'm sure this kind of thing happens all the time." And before I can stop her, she's out of the dressing area and onto the main floor, summoning Susie, even though she just sent her away.

"This is so embarrassing," I whisper to Mel before following her obediently out of the dressing room. I mean, who gets a dress stuck on them?

"Well," Susie says when she appears. "It seems as if you're stuck in this dress! I'll have to get my manager." She crosses her arms, purses her lips, and then takes off into the backroom.

"Sorry," I call after her.

"Don't apologize," Lexi instructs. "It's her *job*." She plops down onto the couch next to Greg/Ryan.

"You look really beautiful, Devon," Greg/Ryan says. "You should get that dress."

"Thanks," I say. "If I can ever get it off." I stand in front of the full length, three-sided mirror and wait for Susie to return with her boss. I take a deep breath and close my eyes. I'm sure I'll be able to take it off. I mean, come on! No one's ever gotten stuck in a dress forever. That's silly. I'm so nervous about the dress, that at first I don't even realize that Lexi and Mel have gone all quiet.

It's only when I hear a male voice say, "Devon?" that I open my eyes. And then I see Luke, in the reflection of the full-length mirror.

"Oh," I say, turning around. "Hey!" What is Luke doing here? "What are you doing here?"

"I saw Lexi come in here, and I figured I'd say hi to her," he says. "What are *you* doing here? I thought you said you were going to be at your grandma's." And then he spots Greg/Ryan sitting over on the couch, and his face gets all squobbly, like my mom's does when she sees something that she doesn't like.

"Oh, hi, Luke," Greg/Ryan says. He sounds a little

flustered. "I was just here at the mall, and I ran into the girls, so I thought I'd say hi." He looks at Luke nervously. "Just like you!"

"You were at the mall by yourself?" Luke asks, putting his hands on his hips.

"Um, no, my mom's around here somewhere," Greg/Ryan says, smiling. "You?"

"I'm with some friends from soccer." And then he turns back to me, his blue eyes flashing. "I guess your grandma's got canceled?" He says it softly, and it's almost worse than if he were yelling, because it's like he's so upset that he can't even muster up the energy to get angry.

"She wasn't feeling well." But it sounds like a lie even to me. Mel's looking down at her shoes, and Lexi's looking between me and Luke nervously.

Maybe I should just tell Luke the truth. That we decided to get Greg/Ryan to play the part of a crazy person from Mel's new school. That he was never my boyfriend in the first place. That I just made it up because I was weirded out about him and Bailey. He'll understand. He's Luke. He's nice. And sensitive. Although. He'll probably be mad at me for lying. Why, why, *why* did I ever say I had an ex-boyfriend?

"Luke—" I start.

But he's already on his way out of the store. And when I try to run after him, Susie stops me. "Oh, no, missy," she says. "You can't go out of the store in that dress." Then she and her boss spends the next five minutes using a special zipper untangler to get me out of the dress. By the time I'm back into my own clothes, Luke's long gone. And when I try to call him on his cell, he doesn't answer.

chapter thirteen

I guess we're broken up now.

And here's how I know.

The weekend: Send Luke three text messages. He doesn't answer any of them. Send Luke five IMs, all along the lines of, "are you mad/I can explain/let's talk about this," etc. No response, except when he *did* just sign off once while I was in the middle of typing something. Which is pretty rude, when you think about it. And Katie (who kept popping up over my shoulder) was all, "Why did Luke sign off while you were typing to him, Devon?" and I had to make something up about how he really had to go because his mom needed the computer.

Monday: Luke does not meet me at my locker in the morning. When he walks into English, he just takes his seat and doesn't say hello to me. Passes notes with Bailey Barelli. Obviously he's not too upset to do *that*. I spend all of lunch in the library with Mel, debating whether or not I have a right to be mad about this, since he hasn't *actually* broken up with me. We decide it's a gray area, which isn't really helping.

Tuesday: Mel and Lexi go off to the radio station, happy as clams. I get stuck going to mock trial. I am tempted to just go home, but then I realize if I do, Luke will be left all alone with Bailey Barelli. And they will know the reason I'm skipping. What I *really* want to do is go to radio with Lexi and Mel. It sounds so fun, they have the cutest advice show that's starting tomorrow! And I want to meet Dylan. But again, I can't really just leave Luke alone with Barelli. Although it turns out that it doesn't really matter, because Mr. Ikwang puts us into groups, and neither Bailey nor I are in Luke's group.

By Wednesday morning, I. Am. Going. Crazy. I have no idea what is going on with me and Luke! Is it possible that he's just broken up with me and forgotten to let me know? Do people really *do* that? I mean, I've heard of people going on dates and then not ever hearing from the guy again, but those are *dates*, not *boyfriends*.

Plus, to make matters even more complicated, the dance is on Saturday. I'm assuming we're not going, but how can I know? My mom is even taking me shopping after school (I still haven't found a dress, which I'm not even sure matters anymore.)

"You have to ask him," Lexi says. We're sitting in the radio station before school starts. She and Mel are putting the finishing touches on their new radio show, and I'm just hanging out with them, because I don't want to face going upstairs to my locker, where Luke will definitely not be waiting for me.

"I can't just *ask* him," I say. "And besides, I've tried. He's ignoring me." I'm sitting on a stool in front of the big board of buttons in the station. It's one of those stools that spins around and around, so that's what I'm doing. Spinning around and around, the whole studio blurring together in a mix of rainbow colors. I don't even care that it's starting to make me feel a little sick. If I throw up, I can go home for the day.

"Well, that's ridiculous," Lexi says. I think she's pointing her finger at me, but it's hard to tell, what with all the spinning. "Go up to him and ask him! Tell him if he doesn't answer, you'll assume that you're not going. You have a right to know."

"She's right," Mel says. "You totally have a right to know." Hmm. Easy for those two to be all rah-rah women's lib. They're both going to the dance. As if he's reading my mind, the studio door opens and Dylan walks in. I stop spinning so I can get a better look at him. Whoa. Dizzy.

"Oh, sorry," he says. "I didn't know you were in here." He smiles at Mel. "I'll text you later."

"Okay," she says, blushing.

"You guys are so cute together," I say forlornly as Dylan shuts the door. I lay my head down on the table in front of me and wait for my head to stop spinning. "It's too bad that my boyfriend broke up with me right before the dance, otherwise we could all triple date."

One of the dials on the board in front of me pokes into my head, and I sit back up. The radio studio is so fancy. It has a board, and a computer, and some microphones. And Lexi and Mel know how to work it all.

"Welcome to Gossipin' Girls with Mel and Lex," Mel says into the microphone. Then she pushes a few buttons and plays her voice back. She giggles. "It sounds cool, doesn't it?"

"Yes," I say, even sadder. "That's the name of your show? How come you're using 'Lex' instead of 'Lexi'?"

"Goes better with Mel," Lexi explains. She pops her gum. "If you were in radio, it could be 'Mel, Lex, and Dev.'"

"That has a nice ring to it," I say. It does, too. Of course, it will never happen. I can't quit mock trial now, definitely not. It doesn't even matter if Luke and Bailey talk, because he's obviously not talking to me anymore. But if I quit, it will just show that they're affecting me. I lay my head down on the counter. This sucks.

After school. My mom drags me to the mall, where she is very happily chattering on and on about how I'm going to be getting a new dress. I know she wants me to be happy, but I don't have the heart to tell her that I don't have a date. Especially since she and Mel's mom have conferred, and after numerous calls to Lexi's mom (where Mrs. Cortland must have been at least a little bit nicer), they have decided we should be allowed to go to the party at Lexi's. Before and after, as long as we're home by eleven.

"What do you think of this one?" my mom asks. We're in H&M, and she's holding up a very heinous-looking green dress, with a drop waist and long sleeves.

Leave it to my mom to find the one horrible dress in the store and suggest I try it on.

"Mom," I say. "Can we please go to the juniors section?" I grab her arm and start pulling her upstairs.

"Okay, okay," she says, laughing up the escalator as she almost steps on my feet. "I'm sorry."

And then I see it. Over in the corner, hanging on a hanger. It's a black dress, fitted on the top, and then all poufed out on the bottom, like a princess in a fairy tale. It has some tulle and lace underneath, puffing the whole thing out, with shades of turquoise and rose woven through, giving the dress a touch of color.

"This is it!" I exclaim, running over. "This is the one!"

"This one?" my mom says, not looking very convinced. "Are you sure you want something so . . . poufy?"

"Mom, I love poufy," I tell her. I pluck the dress off the rack, then grab her hand and start dragging her toward the fitting rooms before she can change her mind. "Poufy is *very* in."

"Okay." She still sounds uncertain.

Once I'm in the dressing room, I tear off my clothes and pull the dress down over my head. Ohmigod. I love, love, love it. It's gorgeous. It brings out the color in my eyes, makes me look super tall, and as I turn around and swish, the lights overhead bounce off all the sparkly material underneath.

And then I start to feel a little bit sad. What's the sense of having this amazing dress if I'm not even going to be going to the dance? But then I realize—why *can't* I go to the dance? Who cares if Luke doesn't want to go with me? I can still go! I can hang with Lexi and Mel and some other people from school. Why should I just stay at home, curled up on the couch watching *My Super Sweet Sixteen* while everyone else is having fun? I'll show them! I'll show up in this fab dress and SHOW THEM! I fling the door open, ready to start showing them by, um, showing my dress to my mom.

"Oh, Devon," my mom says. "It's gorgeous!" She brings her hands to her mouth and starts to get all choked up. Why are parents always getting so worked up over silly things like a dress for a school dance? She hugs me.

"Well," she says, pulling away. "I was hoping to make a whole day of this, but I guess since you found your dress already—"

"We can go grab something to eat," I say. "And of course there's always shoes and accessories." I definitely need new earrings for this dress. And some sparkly silver shoes. And maybe an ankle bracelet.

"Right," my mom says. "Well, why don't you get dressed, and I'll meet you at the register?"

I change out of the dress and back into my street clothes, starting to come down from my new dress high. I mean, it is a *little* bit sad to think about the fact that Luke is never going to see me in it. Well. Actually, maybe he will see me in it. I mean, just because he and I aren't going together, doesn't mean that he won't be there. I'm still going. So maybe he still is, too. Ohmigod. What if he's going with someone else? He wouldn't do that, would he? Invite someone else?

And that's when I open the dressing room door to find Bailey Barelli standing outside one of the stalls. She's wearing a black miniskirt over leggings, and a tight black button-up shirt. Her hair is loose and flowing.

"Oh, hi, Devon," she says, giving me a huge grin. Kim Cavalli is behind her, her arms full of dresses. Ugh. As if running into Barelli wasn't enough, now I have to run into Kim, too? It's like getting a sore throat on top of a really bad headache.

"Hey, guys," I say.

Kim just sniffs.

"Trying on dresses for the dance?" Bailey asks. Her

voice is sweet, but she's totally not fooling me.

"Yup," I say. I hold up the dress I've decided on. "I actually just figured out what I'm going to be wearing, so . . ." I try to push past them, but there's two of them and only one of me, so they're taking up much more space.

"That's a nice dress," Bailey says, flipping her long dark hair back over her shoulder. "What do you think, Kim?"

"It's nice," Kim says. "I like the bottom."

"Thanks," I say. Wow. Are Kim and Bailey actually being nice to me? Maybe now that Luke and I are broken up, they feel sorry for me, and aren't threatened by me anymore. I can't decide if this should make me happy, sad, or mad.

"I guess since now you and Luke are broken up, you're probably under even more pressure to look amazing," Bailey says. She reaches out and touches my arm. "How are you doing with all that?"

"I'm okay," I say, shrugging like it's no big deal. "Junior high relationships aren't really meant to last." I narrow my eyes. "You guys should know that." I'm referring, of course, to Bailey's own relationship with Luke, and to Kim's currently off-again relationship with Matt Connors. But just in case she doesn't get it,

I say, "You know, Kim, like you and Matt breaking up again. You bounced back from that, didn't you?"

Kim narrows her eyes at me. "Of course I did," she says. "Matt Connors is a total loser." She opens her mouth to say something else, but Bailey cuts her off.

"Well, I'm sure it's for the best." She gives me a big smile, showing off her perfect white teeth. "Luke said it had something to do with your ex-boyfriend Greg, so it's great that you two are back together."

"Yeah," I say, not bothering to correct her. "Really great." And before she can say anything else, I turn on my heel and head out of the dressing rooms.

The rest of the week passes pretty uneventfully, except for two major things:

1. My dad works late two times. Both times, he comes rushing in after dinner, gives my mom a kiss on the cheek, and is totally oblivious to the death glare I'm giving him.

2. I bump into Luke in the hallway, and he says, "Sorry," and puts his hands on my shoulders. But that's it. Nothing else. No "I want to break up with you," or "We need to talk," or "Are you confused about what's going on with us, too?" I'm starting to think that if he said, "I hate you and never want to speak to you again,

you're a lying little jerk," I'd be a little bit relieved, since at least then I'd KNOW.

By the time Saturday night rolls around, I'm not really feeling like going to the dance. My new-dress high is pretty much nonexistent. Not to mention that the day after the dance, I'm supposed to be going on a mock trial field trip. Which means that on Sunday, I will have to get up early, get onto a bus, and drive to Westland High School, which is two towns away, to watch their team compete in a mock trial competition.

Even though I feel miserable, I decide that I have to go to the dance, and that if I have to go to the dance, I at least have to look the part. So I load up the bathtub with vanilla and lavender bath salts, light some candles all around the tub, and soak for a long time. I wash my hair with a plumeria shampoo, and give myself a hot conditioning treatment.

"Hello," Katie says, coming in while I'm standing in front of the bathroom mirror after my bath. I'm wrapped up in the fluffy pink robe that my grandma got me last year for my birthday, waiting for the conditioning treatment that's on my hair to finish hot conditioning me up.

"You should knock," I tell her.

"You shouldn't keep the door unlocked if you don't want people coming innnnn," she sings. This makes no sense, but I don't bother correcting her.

"Want to see my curling?" she asks.

The deep conditioning treatment is about to drip down over my forehead and into my eye, so I grab a tissue and wipe off the excess.

"You want to curl my hair?" I ask. "I don't think so. But maybe I'll let you paint my nails." Katie's surprisingly good with nail polish. It might be all those paint by numbers that she does.

"No, Devon," Katie says. "My curling. For the Olympics!" She holds up a teapot and a broom. "Haven't you ever heard of curling? It is an Olympic sport played on the ice."

I've actually never heard of it, but when it comes to the Olympics, in Katie I trust. "That's great," I say. "But you better put mom's antique teapot back before she flips out."

"Okay," Katie says agreeably. She bends down and carefully sets the teapot down on the bathroom floor. "I'd like to do your nails, please." So I let Katie paint my nails. Like I said, she's surprisingly good at nail painting, even if it takes her forever. She paints them a dark magenta to match the underside of my dress, and

I flip through magazines with my free hand. It's almost like being at the salon.

When my nails are done, I rinse out my conditioning treatment, then blow-dry my hair. I consider putting it up in hot rollers so that it will fall around my shoulders in waves, but then I realize that's what Barelli does, and I don't want to copy her. Hers must be natural, though. No way she has time to do that every single day. In the end, I settle on putting my hair up into a twisty ponytail, with some strands falling softly around my face. I use a light purple eye shadow, a pink lip gloss, and put some body glitter on my shoulders.

Then I head downstairs to where my mom is waiting with the camera.

"Are you ready, honey?" she asks. "Where's Luke?"

"Mom, I told you," I say. "He's just going to meet me at Lexi's, his mom didn't have time to pick him up from his dad's house and bring him here first." This is sort of a lie. I mean, Luke is going to be at Lexi's. (This info came from Lexi, who heard it from Jared, who heard it from Luke.) But he's not going to be meeting me. In fact, he probably won't even be talking to me.

"Oh," my mom says. "Right. Well, let me take a few pictures of you, then."

I pose for her in front of the fireplace. Katie comes

over in her curling outfit, which is actually a little bit okay, since it's only a pair of overalls and a heavy winter jacket. Definitely not as bizarre as wearing a pink tutu or a swimming cap in the winter.

Then Katie, my mom, and I all pile into the car so that she can take me over to Lexi's house.

"Now, Katie and I are going to be at a movie and out to dinner," she says. "But your dad will be home, so if you need anything, just call the house."

"Mom, it's going to be fine," I say as we pull into Lexi's driveway. Through the front window of her house, I can see the shadows of people moving around in there. "Well!" I say brightly. "Thanks for the ride. Lexi's mom is going to bring everyone home, and I'll definitely make sure I'm home before eleven." I unbuckle my seat belt and open my door.

"Oh," my mom says. "I think I should walk you in, you know, so that I can talk to Lexi's mom."

"What?" I gasp in horror. "Why? I thought you already talked to her?"

"Plus I want to get a picture of you and Luke." My mom unbuckles her seat belt, and before I can stop her, she's marching up Lexi's steps and ringing the doorbell, Katie hot on her heels.

I follow them slowly, wondering how this is going

to turn out, and knowing that no matter what, it's not going to be good.

Jared opens Lexi's front door. "Oh, hey, Devi," Jared says. My mom frowns at the use of the word "Devi."

"Hey," I say weakly. Suddenly I feel very hot in my dress, like I might faint. I fan myself with my hand, hoping that might help a little. It totally doesn't.

"Hello," my mom says. "I'm Devon's mom."

"Hi, Mrs. Delaney," Jared says. He gives my mom a big grin. "It's so nice to meet you."

"Nice to meet you, too," my mom says. I can tell she's impressed by his manners.

He opens the door to let us in, and thankfully, by some miracle, Lexi's mom is in the living room with everyone. I've spent a lot of time at Lexi's (last summer when I stayed at my grandma's I practically lived there), and it's very rare for Lexi's mom to be visually present when I'm over there. There's a table set up in the middle of the room with a few snacks on it, and music coming from the big screen TV on the wall, which is showing videos.

"Devi!" Lexi calls, rushing over toward me and grabbing me in a hug. "I'm so glad you're here."

Over her shoulder, I can see Luke standing in the corner, talking to Dylan and drinking something out of a paper cup. He's wearing black pants and a gray button-up shirt, and shiny black shoes. He looks amazing. Our eyes meet for a second, but then Luke looks away and goes back to his conversation.

Mel comes up to me, looking gorgeous. She's wearing the long green skirt Lexi gave her, with a white gauzy shirt over a lavender camisole. "Hey," she says. "I need to talk to you." She looks nervous. She spots my mom, and then lowers her voice, "Later. Alone."

"What's going on?" I ask, but Mel shakes her head. Oh, geez. What now? But I don't have time to think too much about whatever Mel has to talk to me about, because I have bigger problems, i.e., getting rid of my mom before she completely and totally embarrasses me.

"Hello, Marcia," Lexi's mom says, walking over to us.

"Oh, hello," my mom says.

"Hello!" Katie pipes up from somewhere around my mom's knees.

"Hi." Lexi's mom looks at Katie warily. I don't think Mrs. Cortland knows what to make of Katie. One time a few weeks ago, when I got stuck babysitting for Katie, Mrs. Cortland drove us both to the mall with Lexi, and Katie was wearing a bathing suit covered in glitter, which she called her ice skating warm-up. I think Mrs. Cortland found the whole thing very strange.

"I just wanted to come in and make sure again that you know Devon needs to be home by eleven," my mom says. "Of course, if there's a problem getting her home by that time, either her father or I would be glad to pick her up."

"No, no, that will be fine," Mrs. Cortland says. How completely embarrassing! I mean, it's fine, eleven o'clock, whatever. But to come in and have to say this in front of all my friends? Luckily Jared is over by the TV, mumbling something about hooking up the Wii, and Luke and Dylan are over in the corner, still ensconced in conversation. So the only people I really need to worry about are Lexi and Mel, and they already know my mom is crazy.

"Okay, Mom!" I say brightly. I give her a hug and a pat on the back. "So I'll see you at eleven then!" I put my hand on the small of her back and very gently guide her toward the door.

"Wait a second," my mom protests. "I want to get a picture of you and Luke."

"Oh, no," I say. "That won't be necessary, I—"

"Devon, don't be embarrassed," my mom says. "Yoohoo, Luke!" she calls over to where Luke is standing with Dylan. "Would you mind coming over here so that I can get a picture of you and Devon?" Ohmigod, ohmigod, ohmigod, my mom did not just say that. My mom did not just attempt to get a picture of me and the boy who broke up with me.

"Mom," I say. "Really, I—"

"Okay," Luke says. He puts his drink down on a table and comes over to where I'm standing with my mom. Ohmigod. What? Why? Why is he coming over?

"Lean in close and smile!" my mom instructs. Luke leans in close to me, and I can smell the cologne he's wearing. His slides his arm around my shoulder, pulling me ever closer, and my stomach does a flip.

"So I guess you didn't tell your mom we broke up?" Luke whispers into my ear.

"No," I say. "I didn't tell her." And then I start to get a little mad. I mean, why would I tell my mom we broke up when Luke didn't even tell *me*? "And besides, I didn't know if we really broke up, since you refuse to talk to me."

"I didn't refuse to talk to you," Luke says. "I was just taking some time to sort out my thoughts."

"Yeah, well, you could have at least told me that."

"Smile!" my mom says. She puts the camera down and looks at us in frustration. "Guys, you're not smiling!"

"Say cheese!" Katie yells, bouncing around on one foot. "Say cheese and your face will go into a smile!"

I force myself to smile, and Luke does the same. After what seems like a bazillion shots, my mom puts the camera away, kisses me goodbye, and heads out the door, Katie in tow.

"Anyway," I say to Luke once they're gone, trying to sound haughty, "Thanks for taking a picture with me." I turn on my heel and start making my way over to where Mel and Lexi are standing in the corner, but he stops me.

"Devon," he says, grabbing my hand and pulling me back toward him. "I'm sorry that I blew you off." He sighs and drops his eyes to the floor. "It was stupid of me to do that, but I just didn't know what to say. Seeing you there with Greg, it just . . ." He sighs. "I dunno."

"I'm sorry about that," I say. "But there's nothing going on between me and Ryan."

"Who's Ryan?" Luke frowns. Shoot.

"I mean Greg," I correct.

"But you were at the mall with him," Luke says. "I saw you there. You lied to me."

"Yeah, but we just ran into him," I say. "We were just at the mall, you know, shopping, and we ran into him."

Luke frowns. "Then why didn't you just say that

as soon as I saw you?" he says. "And besides, you told me you were going to your grandmother's."

"I *was* there," I say. "But then I went to the mall. I needed to get a dress for the dance, and I wanted to surprise you."

"You were at your grandmother's? And you expect me to believe that you didn't run into Greg there and ask him to go to the mall with you?"

What is he—Oh. Right. Greg supposedly lives near my grandmother's house.

"I didn't invite him!" I say. "He just—"

"He just happened to be at a mall really far away from where he lives?"

"No," I say. My head is spinning, and I'm trying to keep track of all the lies. "It wasn't . . . I don't . . ." Ahhh!

"Yeah," he says. "That's what I thought." He turns and starts to walk away.

"Wait," I say, grabbing his arm and pulling him back toward me. "We need to talk."

He doesn't say anything, so I rush on before he can shut me down, "Maybe after the dance we could go back to my house or something?"

Luke sighs and runs his fingers through his hair. I hold my breath and hope he'll say yes.

LAUREN BARNHOLDT

I need to tell Luke the truth. Even though it's going to be hard, I need to tell him and see if he'll forgive me. There's no other way.

"Okay," he says finally. "After the dance."

I just hope it's not too late.

Half an hour later, we're all in Lexi's mom's Hummer, heading over to the dance. I'm sitting in the back, next to Mel, and we're having a whispered conversation, because Mel has a big scandal going on.

Apparently, her mom, still stuck on the whole idea of her going to private school, but not being so happy with the whole Corbin thing, decided to call the school and ask some questions. And when she found out that there was no Corbin enrolled at St. Mary's (I knew we should have used Ethan!), she confronted Mel about it. Mel tried to deny it, but finally she broke down and told her the truth. Mel is very good at keeping secrets, but she is not a very good liar.

"You told her that Corbin was a decoy?" I exclaim.

"Yes," she says. She plays with the silver ring that's around her middle finger. "I told her that I didn't want to go to private school, and that I had to resort to drastic measures."

"And what did she say about that?"

"She said that since I pulled a stunt like this, it just proved that I need to go to private school even more than she thought." Mel sighs. "So it looks like I'm going."

"What?!" I shriek. "Mel, no!" I can't lose my boyfriend and my best friend all in one week.

"There's nothing I can do," Mel says. "I tried, and she found out, and now it's over." She looks down at her hands sadly. "We can still hang out after school. And on weekends." I'm getting choked up, and so is Mel, and I can tell if we keep talking about it, we're probably both going to start crying.

"We'll think of something," I say, and squeeze her hand reassuringly as Lexi's mom pulls up in front of the school.

The gym is decorated all in black and white, with balloons and streamers lazily crisscrossing their way across the ceiling. There's a huge table set up in the back, with cookies and punch, along with pizza and pieces of cake. Music is blaring out of enormous speakers that are set up on the stage, and there's a booth in the back where people who don't want to dance can play Rock Band on PlayStation.

I'm not really that hungry, but I *am* a little thirsty, so I head over to the table in the back to get a cup of punch, and Mel follows me. Hopefully I don't spill it on myself. I don't have the best record with red beverages—one time I spilled a whole pitcher of cherry Kool-Aid all over my new white sneakers.

There's a fast song playing, and Lexi immediately grabs Jared's hand and pulls him onto the dance floor. I lost sight of Luke once we got into the gym, so I have no idea where he is. I did hope he would ask me to dance, but maybe later. I mean, he wouldn't have agreed to talk to me later if he wasn't at least a little bit interested in staying together, right?

Mel plucks a cupcake off the platter and takes a big bite. "Wow, these are good."

I pour myself a drink, making sure to fill my paper cup up only halfway. Even so, some punch threatens to slosh out of the cup and onto my hand. "But, um, Mel, why aren't you over there with Dylan?" Dylan's leaning against the wall on the side of the gym, talking to some kid I don't recognize.

Now that I think about it, I haven't seen Mel talk to Dylan once tonight. At Lexi's house, Dylan was mostly talking to Luke, and in the car, Mel decided to sit with me. Is Mel just being nice because she knows I'm at the dance by myself?

"Mel," I say, "you don't have to babysit me, I'm totally fine." It's true. I am actually kind of fine. I don't mind hanging out by the food table. I'll be able to keep an eye on Luke, which is fab.

"I don't mind," Mel says breezily. She gulps down some punch. "I like hanging out with you. Besides, there's no way I'd leave you all alone." Hmmm. Something in her tone doesn't sound like she's doing this just to be friendly. I set my punch down on the table.

"Mel," I say. "Something in your tone doesn't sound like you're hanging out with me just to be friendly."

"What do you mean?" But a guilty look crosses her face. Mel really is a bad liar.

"What's the deal?"

"What deal?"

"The reason you and Dylan aren't talking at all? Did you have a fight or something?" Must be something going around. Everyone's fighting. Me and Luke, Dylan and Mel . . . at least Lexi and Jared are okay. I watch them go sliding by on the dance floor, dancing to a slow song. Lexi's head is on his shoulder, and she has her eyes closed.

"Bathroom conference," I say to Mel, and before she can protest, I've grabbed her hand and am dragging her to the bathroom in the corner of the gym. Once we're in there, I check every stall to make sure no one is listening. Eww. These bathrooms really could use a good cleaning. I mean, there's toilet paper all over the floor.

"Now," I say, emerging from the last stall and kicking a piece of toilet paper off my shoe. "Tell me what's going on."

"I don't know what you're talking about." Mel bites her lip, which is a telltale sign that she's hiding something.

"You're biting your lip," I tell her.

"No, I'm not," she says, still biting.

"Yes, you are. Now tell."

"Well, I just . . . I don't know what to say to him."

"What do you mean you don't know what to say to him?" I frown. "Don't you guys talk all the time in radio?" I catch a look at myself over Mel's shoulder in the full-length mirror on the wall of the bathroom. It's a shame that this night is such a disaster and I'm here by myself, because my dress really is super cute. I purse my lips and smooth down my hair.

"Well, yeah, but that's different. We have . . . I don't know, like we're doing things that necessitate us talking." I give her a skeptical look, and she rushes on. "Like if I want to talk to him about a story idea I have! Or if I want to ask him advice on how to run the board, that kind of thing!"

"Then why can't you talk to him about radio now?" I ask. I move past her to the mirror, then reach into my bag and pull out my lip gloss. I reline my lips and then blot, smiling into the mirror to make sure I don't have any on my teeth.

"Oh, yeah, I'm sure he wants to talk about radio at the dance," Mel says. Hmm. Good point. I mean, the whole point of the dance is to do something kind of romantic. You don't want to be reminded of school.

"But it's at least as a way to start a conversation," I offer. I hold out my lip gloss, and Mel takes it, stepping in front of the mirror to put it on.

"What's going on in here?" Lexi asks, walking into the bathroom. "I have been looking for you two all over the place."

"You have?" I ask.

"Yes." Lexi takes out a small curling iron from her purse, and plugs it into the outlet on the wall. "I need a touch-up," she explains. "Anyway," she goes on. "I don't think it's right that you two are basically ignoring your dates. I mean, Luke's been in the Rock Band booth all night, and Dylan's been stuck talking to that boring kid from our science class." Her eyebrows knit together in concentration. "What's his name? Brutus?"

"Brandon." Brandon's Lexi's lab partner. She really should pay better attention in class.

She picks up the curling iron and starts to curl the bottom of her hair.

"And Luke's not my date," I say. "So I could care less if he's in the Rock Band booth." Not exactly true, but whatever.

"And if Dylan wants to talk to me so bad, he knows where to find me," Mel says.

"In the girls' bathroom?" Lexi looks skeptical.

Mel shrugs.

"Girls!" Lexi says. "I'm serious! I don't like all this hiding from boys. If you want something done, go out there and do it!"

I'm not sure exactly what she's talking about, getting things done. I mean, I *do* want to talk to Luke, but that's really not supposed to be happening until later. Still, I get the point of what she's trying to say. But I try to pretend that she's just referring to Mel, even though I'm just as guilty.

"She's right," I say to Mel. "You should go out there and talk to him."

"What about you?" Mel challenges. "You should be out there talking to Luke."

"Wellll," I say. "That's different." I try to sound breezy, like I don't care that Luke is in the Rock Band booth, while I'm in here hiding from him. I reach into my bag and pull out my eye shadow, scooting in next to Lexi and brushing some over my eyelid. "I mean, Luke isn't talking to me, so . . ." I shrug, as if the whole thing is out of my hands.

"Aren't you guys supposed to talk about your relationship after the dance?" Lexi asks. She's winding up the cord of her curling iron and putting it back into her bag.

"How did you know about that?" I ask.

"Jared told me." She shrugs, like it's not earth-shattering news that she's just delivered.

"How did Jared know?" I ask.

"Because Luke told him."

"He did?" I drop the eye shadow brush and it bounces off the counter and into the sink. Eww. I reach in and fish it out, then drop it into the garbage. No way I'm using that again.

"Yeah." Lexi shrugs again.

"Well, what did he say exactly?" This information is very important. Maybe he told Jared something that he's planning on doing. Like breaking up with me. Or maybe he said he's going to forgive me. Or maybe . . .

"He said 'Luke said him and Devon are going to be talking after the dance.'"

"That's it?" And Lexi didn't think she should pump him for information? What is wrong with her? "What is wrong with you?" I demand. "Why didn't you pump him for information?"

"I dunno," Lexi says. "I figured it was your business." This, from someone who's planning on broadcasting an advice show every day at school.

"You know," Mel says suddenly. "Lexi's right." Uh-oh. Mel has this tone in her voice, the same tone she had last year when they tried to tell Mazie Livingston that she couldn't be on the boys wrestling team. Mel led this whole campaign with posters and everything.

"She is?" I say nervously, not sure what's coming.

"Yes!" Mel throws up her hands. "This is ridiculous, sitting in the bathroom while everyone is out there having fun."

"True," I say.

"I need to get out there and have fun with my date. Who cares if it's a little bit awkward? How am I going to know if we really like each other if I never even try to talk to him?" She's pacing now, and her voice is kind of shrieky. Honestly, I'm a little scared of her. "Middle school dances are *supposed* to be awkward!" She grabs me by the shoulders. "Devon!"

"Yes?" I try.

"Are you with me?" She gives me a little shake.

"Um . . . I don't really—"

"I said ARE. YOU. WITH. ME?"

"Yes!" I say suddenly. "I'm with you!" And I am. All I have to do is tell Luke the truth. He's Luke! He's nice! And maybe he'll be a little mad and weirded out at first, but he did agree to talk to me later. And he even said himself that he wasn't ignoring me because he wanted to break up. He just needed some time!

So as Mel heads out into the dance to find Dylan and attempt to strike up a conversation with him, I head out into the dance to pry Luke away from the Rock Band booth and tell him the truth about Greg/Ryan. And Lexi goes out to find Jared, probably so they can make out in a corner somewhere.

When I get to the Rock Band booth, a very rude kid informs me that there's a line to play the game.

"Oh, I don't want to play," I say. "I just want to know if you've seen Luke Nichols?"

"Never heard of him," the kid says, waving his hand. The line to play isn't really that long. It's not even really a line, but more like a huddle of people waiting. And Luke's not in it.

I head out of the booth and wander back over to the table. Maybe Luke's in the bathroom or something. I pick up a cookie so that I have something to do with my hands, and let my eyes scan the crowd. I spot Mel over in a corner, standing by Dylan. They're not really talking, but then he leans in and whispers something to her, and she laughs, tilting her head back and letting her hair fall down around her shoulders.

I see Lexi dancing with Jared again, her head against his shoulders. And then, as my eyes move across the dim room, I see Luke. The overhead light washes over him, and in that moment, I just have this feeling that everything's going to be okay.

I put one foot forward, about to make my way through the throng of dancing kids to get to him. Until I realize what he's doing.

Dancing. With Bailey Barelli.

chapter fourteen

For a second, I don't move. His arms are around her waist, and she's talking to him, and he's laughing about something, and before I can even think about what I'm doing, I'm pushing through the crowd and out of the gym. The lights overhead are making shadow patterns on the floor, and I'm looking down, concentrating on making my sparkly shoes move toward the door. I thought he wanted to talk later? I thought maybe there was a chance, that maybe he could forgive me, but now . . . I reach into my bag and pull out my cell phone.

I need to call my mom, I need her to pick me up, I need to get out of here.

I dial her number, but it goes right to her voice mail. Figures. She's probably in the movie with Katie.

I call my dad at home, but I get the answering machine, so I hang up and dial his cell. "Devon?" my dad asks when he answers. "Is everything okay?"

"Yeah," I say, trying to slow my beating heart. "Well, sort of. The thing is, I want to come home." I sit down on a bench on the sidewalk outside the gym.

"You want to come home?" he asks incredulously. I can't blame him. I mean, I did beg and beg to be able to go to this dance.

"Yes," I say.

"Right now?"

"Yes," I say. "Right now please."

"Why?" he asks.

"No reason," I say, not really wanting to get into it. "It's just that, um, my stomach is a little bit upset." I stand up and move around a little bit. God, it's cold out. I really should have listened to my mom when she said I should wear a coat. But honestly, who wants to wear a coat when your dress is this cute? Of course, if I'd known I'd be running out of the dance and forced to stand in the cold while waiting for my dad to come and get me, I would have reconsidered.

"Are you sure?" he says. "This isn't going to be one of those things where I get there to pick you up and you decide you want to stay, is it? Because I'm kind of in the middle of something." For the first time I realize there are voices in the background of wherever my dad is. It sounds like he's at some kind of party or something.

"In the middle of what?" I ask suspiciously.

"I'm just . . . uh, I'm out. At a work thing." Yeah, right. Work thing my butt. Sounds like he's out with Stephanie. I feel the tears welling up in my eyes, but what choice do I have? I can't get ahold of my mom, so it's either having my dad come to pick me up, or going back into the dance. Which I so do not want to do.

"Dad," I say, pleading.

"Okay," he says. "I'll be there in ten minutes."

Ten minutes? Where is he, Antarctica?

I stand outside, wondering if I'm going to be able to get out of here before Mel or Lexi realize I'm gone. Once I get in my dad's car, I'll send them a text letting them know where I am so they don't worry, but for right now, I don't really want to talk to anyone. I walk around in circles a little bit, trying to stay warm.

"Devon." I hear his voice before I see him. Luke. Calling my name from behind me.

"Oh," I say, turning around. "Yeah?"

"I saw you run out here, and I just wanted to make sure everything's okay." The door to the school shuts behind him, and he moves a little closer to me.

I almost laugh. "Yeah, like you care."

"What's that supposed to mean?"

"Luke, it's fine," I say. "I get it. You and I broke up, and now you're getting back with Barelli. You don't have to come out here and try to make me feel better. I'm perfectly fine, and in fact, I'm only going home because my stomach is bothering me." I put my hand on my stomach to make it a little bit more believable.

"You're going home?" he asks.

"Because my stomach is bothering me," I repeat. "Now please, just go away." I turn my back on him, walking a few feet away, and hoping that I don't start crying while he's out here.

"Go away?" he asks incredulously. "You want me to go away? Devon, you're the one who wanted to talk to me after the dance."

"Oh, okay," I say, whirling back around. "So now you decide you're ready to talk to me, so I'm just supposed to be super excited about it? After you ignored me for over a week? Sorry, Luke, I can't just go back and forth that easily." I cross my arms, daring him to come closer.

"*You're* mad at *me*?" he asks. "That's really great. You go off hanging out with your ex-boyfriend without even telling me, and *you're* mad at *me.*"

"You were in there dancing with Bailey!" I throw my hands up in the air and point to the gym. "And it looked pretty intense. After you *said* that we were going to talk after the dance!"

"Yeah," he says, his eyes flashing. "And the only reason I started dancing with her is because she said you were getting back together with Greg. Which I already *knew,* since I saw you two at the mall after you lied about being at your grandma's."

"She said what?" I gasp. God, can that girl get any more up in my business? And why would she say that? Up until this point, she's just been super annoying, but I guess it was only a matter of time until she started lying about things. Those types always do. Then I remember running into Bailey and Kim that day in the dressing room, while I was getting my dress. How Bailey said she'd heard I'd gotten back together with Greg, and how I hadn't bothered to correct her, because I didn't want her to think that I was heartbroken over Luke. Oh, for God's sake.

"He's not my ex-boyfriend!" I say, the words tumbling out into the night air before I can stop them. "He's just a guy who was pretending to be my ex-boyfriend."

"What?" Luke takes a step back, looking confused.

"Yeah, that's right," I say, throwing my hands up into the air. "I made him up!"'

"You made *what* up about him?" Luke still looks confused, his eyebrows knit together in concentration as he tries to wrap his mind around this new bit of info.

"No, *him*," I say. "I made *him* up. I've never had an ex-boyfriend, Luke. He's one of Lexi's friends, a guy she knows from her old school."

"And you hired him to pretend to be your boyfriend?" Luke asks incredulously.

"Not exactly," I say, swiping at my tears with the back of my hand. "He did it for free."

"Why would you do something like that?" he asks, and the way he says it makes me feel like he thinks I'm crazy. Which, I guess, looking back on it, I kind of am. I mean, it *is* pretty crazy to do something like that. Just make up that you have an ex-boyfriend. Especially when it isn't even the *first time* you've done something like that. I have more fake boyfriends than I've had real boyfriends.

"Because of Barelli," I say. "You guys were passing notes back and forth and texting and the four-wheeling!"

"The four-wheeling?" He's confused.

"Yeah, the four-wheeling! At her uncle's farm, where apparently you two would hang out on the weekends and just have so much fun."

"Devon, we went there like twice."

"And how was I supposed to know that?" I ask him. And now I'm crying, tears streaming down my face, and I'm cursing myself for not paying the extra money for waterproof makeup, but honestly, who could have foreseen this? Not me.

"Maybe if you'd asked me, if you'd—"

"You should have told me! You should have made me feel better! I was your girlfriend!"

"I would have if you asked. And it doesn't change the fact that you lied to me."

My dad pulls up then. I haven't noticed, but it's started drizzling, and the wipers of the car are making little squeaky sounds on the windshield.

"It doesn't matter now," I say sadly, looking down at my hands. In my heart, I know what I want him to say. I want him to tell me it does matter, that we can work it out, that he's not mad at me, that he forgives me for lying, that he doesn't like Bailey. And then I'll go and tell my dad I don't need a ride home after all, and he'll be kind of annoyed, but it won't matter, because

Luke and I will be talking and I'll be able to talk to my dad about it later.

But all Luke says is, "Yeah, I guess it doesn't." And then he turns around and heads back into the dance, and I turn around and head for my dad's car.

"Is everything all right?" my dad asks as I hop into the car. The drizzling outside has made little drops on the skirt of my dress, turning the fabric darker.

"Fine," I say, looking out the window. No way I'm going to be confiding in my *dad* after what just happened. I mean, hello. He's lying to our whole family and definitely *not* my favorite person right now. I decide I hate all men.

"Does this have anything to do with Luke?" my dad asks.

"No," I say. "I told you, I don't feel good."

"So it doesn't have anything to do with the fact that Luke was just standing outside with you, and the two of you looked like you were involved in a very serious conversation?"

"No," I say again. "It has nothing to do with that."

"Okay." There's silence, and so I reach over and switch on the radio, then look out the window and feel sorry for myself.

"Devon," my dad says. "Are you sure there's nothing you want to talk about?"

"Are you sure there's nothing *you* want to talk about?" I counter. Because at this point, you know, I've really had it.

"What do you mean?" he frowns.

"Just what I said," I say. "Do you want to tell me anything?" And even though I know a lot of this has to do with how upset I am about Luke, and how upset I am at myself for not learning my lesson the first time, it feels good to finally confront my dad.

"No," my dad says. He seems very confused.

We're pulling into the driveway now, and part of me just wants to let it go. But as I'm getting out of the car, I turn around and say, "I know about Stephanie." And then I calmly shut the door, head up to my room, and stay in bed for the rest of the night.

For some reason, I wake up at eight o'clock the next morning. Eight o'clock! On a Sunday. I never wake up that early. Ever. I don't like to get out of bed before ten. Otherwise, what's the point of having a weekend? I'm about to roll over and go back to sleep, when the events of the night before come rushing back to me. Luke dancing with Bailey. My confession in the rain.

The ride home with my dad. Me telling him I know about Stephanie, and him not denying it.

I know I'm not going to be able to get back to sleep, and I sigh. The sun is shining through my window. Ugh. I am so not in a sunshiny mood right now. From downstairs, I can hear the low sounds of my parents' voices, and dishes clinking. They must be having breakfast. And from the way they're talking in low voices, I can tell they're talking about something serious.

Is my dad confessing everything? Oh, God. This is so not what I want to deal with today. I decide to stay in my room for the whole day. And then I remember I'm supposed to be going on that mock trial field trip this afternoon. Ugh. I pull the covers over my head and close my eyes. I'm drifting in and out of sleep, and the next thing I know, I hear that the TV in my room is on.

I open my eyes to find Katie sitting on my floor, the TV turned to MSNBC.

"What are you doing in here?" I ask.

"Watching the news," she says. "Today is the big day!" She gets up off the floor and twirls around in a circle. She's still wearing her pajamas, light blue with pink dogs printed all over them.

"What big day?" I ask.

"The day they decide about the big Olympic scandal, Devon. Don't you watch the news?"

"Not really," I say, pulling the covers back over my head. "I have my own problems. Why aren't you watching it downstairs, like a normal person?"

"Because Mommy and Daddy are down there, talking about very important grown-up things."

"Yeah," I say. "I'll bet they are."

"But they are not," Katie reports, "using harsh tones." She does another little twirl. Poor, deluded little Katie. She has no idea that even though my parents aren't using harsh tones, they are in very big trouble. Maybe they'll send me to live with my grandma again. That actually wouldn't be so bad. I could start school out there. I would even know Greg/Ryan. How ironic would that be? If I ended up becoming BFF with the guy who basically ruined my life?

"Are you waking up now?" Katie asks.

"No," I say.

"You seem like you're awake," Katie insists.

"Yeah, well, I'm not," I say. "A lot of things seem to be what they're really not."

Katie wrinkles up her nose. "I don't like that," she says. "It seems like a riddle."

My cell phone rings from the nightstand next to

me, and for a second, my heart hopes that it's Luke. But it's not. It's Mel.

"Devon!" she says. "Oh, thank God, I've been so worried!"

"I'm fine," I say. "Didn't you get my text?" Last night after I was safely in my room, I texted Mel and Lexi to let them know what happened, that I'd gone home with my dad, and that I was okay.

"Yes," she says. "But I was still worried. What happened?"

"Nothing I really want to talk about," I say. I get down under the covers so that Katie won't hear me. "But Luke and I broke up, and I confronted my dad on his affair."

Mel gasps from the other line. "What happened?!" she asks.

"Nothing." I say. "Yet." I snuggle down deeper into the covers. I wonder if I can just stay here forever. Probably not. Especially since I can feel Katie down at the bottom of the bed, sticking her hands under the covers and grabbing my toes. I curl my legs further up into the bed.

"What do you mean, 'yet'?" Mel asks.

"They're downstairs, probably just waiting to have some big talk with me."

"Yeah, well, join the club. My mom is about to have some big talk with me, too, about how I'm off to private school." She sighs, and I feel guilty for a second. All this stuff going on with Luke and my dad, and I totally forgot about Mel being shipped off to private school.

And then I have an idea. "Hey," I say, sitting up in bed. "What are you doing this afternoon? Can I come over before my mock trial thing?"

"Sure," she says. "Although it's not really that fun around here right now, what with my mom being mad at me and all."

"That's okay," I say. "That's actually good. And what about Dylan? What happened last night?"

"Wellll," Mel says slowly. "It was a little bit awkward at first, you know, because I didn't exactly know what I should talk to him about."

"Right," I say.

"But then I just started talking to him about radio, and then we started talking about school stuff, and I told him about how my mom wants to send me to a private school, and he was sooo understanding." There's a long pause. "And then, um, you know, we went back to Lexi's after, and I could swear he was going to kiss me, but then my mom showed up to pick me up, so I don't know."

"Mel, that's amazing!" I say. "Do you think—"

"Devon!" my mom calls from downstairs. "Could you come down here?"

Of course the moment Mel gets to the good part, my mom has to call me down for a conversation which I definitely do not want to have. I sigh and tell Mel I have to go.

"Can I stay in here?" Katie asks. She's sitting cross-legged on my floor.

"Yes," I say. "Just don't mess anything up."

Katie jumps into my bed and into the covers, and I head downstairs. My mom and dad are sitting at the table, looking serious. Ugh. I really wish we did not have to have this conversation. In fact, I wish *everything* that happened last night didn't happen.

"Good morning," my mom says, smiling at me. How can she be smiling at a time like this? "Would you like a waffle?" I notice a big plate of waffles on the table. They actually look delish.

"No thanks," I say, sitting down on the chair across from her. The floor is cold under my feet, and I realize I'm only wearing one sock. How did that happen? I pull it off so that one foot isn't colder than the other.

"So, your father says you know about Stephanie,"

my mom says. She takes a sip of her orange juice, and suddenly, my throat feels dry.

"Yes," I say. I reach across the table for the juice and pour some into my glass.

"I want to ask how you found out, but something tells me I might not like what you have to say," my dad says. Obviously he thinks I did it by spying and treachery, which is pretty much true. But is he upset that I spied, or is he upset that he got found out?

"I agree," my mom says. And there's a silence in which I realize they want me to tell them. It's like one of those leading questions—they're saying they're afraid to know the answer, therefore giving me a chance to prove them wrong by telling them I found out by some innocent maneuvers. Whatev. I don't have anything to hide. If anyone should be upset, it's my dad.

"I saw you with her at the coffee shop." I sip my juice. "You were having coffee with her or something, right before Mom was going to pick up me and Lexi." I shoot him a look, as if to say, *See how close you came to being caught, not so smart, are you?*

"Oh, yeah," my dad says. He turns to my mom. "We were having a coffee between appointments." Aha! So he does work with her! I can't believe he's rubbing it in my mom's face! They were having a coffee between appointments? Does my mom really need to know that stuff? I glare at my dad. But my mom doesn't seem to mind. In fact, she seems totally unbothered by it.

"But how," my mom says to me, "did you know her name was Stephanie?"

Oh. Right.

"I looked in Dad's phone," I announce, almost proudly. Take that! You can't get away with anything on my watch!

"Devon, you shouldn't have done that," my mom says. "You can't go around looking in people's phones. I wouldn't have looked in your phone."

"Well, you shouldn't have lied to me," I say to my dad.

"I didn't lie to you," my dad says. "I just didn't tell you something."

"Didn't you say lying by omission is just as horrible as really lying?" I ask my mom. She did, too. That day I was upset that Luke hadn't told me about how he used to date Bailey. And look how that turned out. She was right. Luke totally still likes Bailey.

"Well." She looks nervously at my dad and takes another sip of her juice. "Yes, I did, but in this case, it's a little different."

"Honey, the reason we didn't tell you is because we didn't want you to get all worked up over nothing. We wanted to make sure everything worked out before we told you and Katie, so that you wouldn't get upset and start asking all sorts of questions," my dad says.

I almost choke on my juice. "You knew about this?" I ask my mom incredulously. Ohmigod. How ridiculous is this! My mom and dad wanted to make sure it worked out with my dad and Stephanie before telling us? So that it wouldn't upset us? How crazy are they?

"Of course," my mom says. She reaches for the plate in the middle of the table and drops a waffle onto her plate. "Your father wouldn't buy a house without consulting with me first. Really, Devon." She forks off a piece of waffle and drags it through some syrup before popping it into her mouth.

"Wait, what?" I ask. "Buy a house?" What are they talking about?

"Yes," my dad says. "I wouldn't have started consulting with a realtor without your mom knowing about it. In fact, your mom is the one who brought up the whole moving thing in the first place."

"Stephanie's a realtor?" I exclaim.

"Well, yeah," my mom says. "What did you think she was?"

"Oh, um . . ." I trail off, not sure if I should tell them. What would I say? *I thought you were having an*

affair with some woman named Stephanie? "Uh, I wasn't exactly sure."

But my mom and dad know what I was thinking without me even needing to say anything. "Oh, Devon," my dad says. "Is that why you ran out of the car like that last night? Because you thought . . ." My dad and mom exchange a glance and then burst out laughing.

"It's not funny," I protest. "It was very psychologically taxing, thinking that your father was having an affair!"

"Why didn't you just ask me?" my dad wants to know.

"Because," I say, "I didn't know how to bring it up." Suddenly, I'm starving. Now that I know everything's okay between my parents, my appetite is back full force. I take three waffles off of the plate and put them on my own. Mmm. I slather them with butter and syrup, and then eat a piece. Wow. I wonder how my mom was able to pull these off. They taste amazing, all buttery and rich. I'm so consumed with the buttery goodness of the waffles that for a second, I forget that my parents have just dropped another bombshell.

"Hey, wait a minute," I say. "What do you mean, we're moving?" I put my fork down next to my plate.

"We're thinking of getting a bigger house," my mom explains. She gets up and takes her plate to the sink. "Now that I'm making a bit more money off of my web design business, we're at the point where we can finally afford it." She returns to the table and reaches out and grabs my dad's hand.

"So now we're moving?" This is ridiculous! I'm going to have to leave all my friends, Mel will already be going to private school, and if I move away, I'm never going to be able to see her. Not to mention I'll lose Lexi.

"Don't worry," my dad says. He drains the rest of his coffee and picks a piece of bacon off his plate and pops it into his mouth. "We made sure that the only houses we look at will be in the school district, so that you don't have to change schools."

Oh. I relax a little. Good. Although now that it's no longer a possibility, I think about how cool it might have been to change schools. Where no one would know who I was, and I wouldn't have to deal with seeing Luke and Bailey together every single day. My stomach does a flop, and suddenly, I'm not hungry anymore. I push my plate away from me and head upstairs to start working on the plan I've come up with to keep Mel out of private school.

chapter fifteen

"What's this?" Mel asks when she opens the door to her house later.

"This!" I announce happily, brushing by her and into the front hall. "Is my plan to save your life!"

I take off my coat and hang it on the coat rack in the hall.

"A computer?" Mel asks, looking skeptically at the laptop I'm holding.

"It's my dad's," I tell her. My dad let me borrow it when I explained my plan to him. Of course, this might have something to do with the fact that I think he was feeling a little bit guilty that I thought he was having an affair for so long. Otherwise he might not have let me borrow it. "Your dad's computer is going to save my life?" Mel asks dubiously.

"Not the computer exactly," I say. "*Me* and the computer!" I'm triumphant. And this better work. I've been slaving away on it all morning.

"How?"

"Well," I say. "I made up a whole PowerPoint presentation on how you can get just as good of an education at a public school as you can at a private school. My dad helped me with it," I admit.

"Devon!" Mel squeals. She jumps up and down in the hallway.

"Well, calm down, you don't have to jump and down, you're going to step on my foot." But I'm excited that she's so excited. "Is your mom home?"

"Yeah," Mel says. "She's in the kitchen."

"Great," I say.

"What's in the bag?" Mel asks, looking at the garment bag I'm holding. I took it out of my dad's closet—it's what all his suits are in when they come back from the dry cleaners. It looks very professional. "My outfit," I say. "Come on."

We head into Mel's room, where I pull out what I have in the bag. Black skirt, chunky gray sweater with a cowl neck, black patterned tights, and black high-heeled shoes. Taken from my mom's closet, with her permission of course.

"You're dressing up like a secretary?" Mel asks.

"These are not frumpy secretary clothes!" I protest. "This skirt is Hermes!"

"It is?"

"Well, no. But it's from H&M, and I saw one almost exactly the same online at Hermes, so . . ." I love H&M. Really, all the bargains can be found there.

"Wait, so what am I supposed to wear? And what happened with your parents?"

I lead Mel to her closet, where I flip through her things, trying to find something that looks profes-sional yet stylish, and fill her in on what happened at breakfast.

"So basically," I say. "Everything's fine."

"So basically," Mel says. "You should have just asked your dad about it, and then maybe this whole thing could have been avoided."

Geez. She doesn't have to rub it in. I mean, yes, I could have asked my dad about it, but then I would have been obsessing over the whole them finding a house thing.

"Well, yeah," I say. "But then I would have no bright side today, on the day when Luke and I are broken up. So at least I can say to myself, 'Well, Devon, at least your parents are fine.'"

Mel looks at me and smiles, and I reach into her closet and pull out a slate gray dress with a cool cut out pattern all around the collar. "How about this?" I ask. "You can wear it with—" And then I notice Mel's face is getting all scrunchy, and her cheeks are getting a little bit blotchy, and the next thing I know, Mel sits down on the floor of her closet and starts to cry.

"Um," I say, not quite sure what this is about. "It's okay, you don't have to wear the dress. Honestly, you don't have to get dressed up at all if you don't want to, it's fine."

"No, no, it's just . . ." Mel sniffs and moves an ice skate out of the way and pats the floor next to her, like she wants me to sit. Hmm. I'm not too sure about this. It's not a walk-in closet or anything, in fact, it's kind of on the small side as closets go, and I'm not sure there's room for Mel, much less the both of us.

"Um, I'm not sure there's room for me in there,"

I say. "Why don't you come out and we can—"

"SIT!" Mel commands. Yikes. Okay, then.

I scooch in next to her and pull my knees up to my chin. Well, I guess there are worse places to be. Like a coffin.

"What's wrong?" I ask Mel.

"It's just . . . everything's changing," Mel says. She sniffs again.

"But we will *always* be friends," I tell her, squeezing her hand. "Always. No matter who lives where or what school we go to or who we're dating or whatever. Always. No matter what."

"Do you promise?" Mel asks.

"I promise." And then I give her a hug, and get ready to save Mel from private school.

I do look pretty cute. I'm just saying. Like, if I were to be going on a job interview right now for some fancy job, I would totally get it. Not that thirteen-year-olds can really get that many fancy jobs, but if we could, I'd be hired. Actually, I could probably get a job that older people could get. I think I look at least sixteen in this outfit. And can't sixteen-year-olds be assistants or something? I think there are a couple of people in my dad's office who work there over the summer who are sixteen. I could definitely get one of those jobs.

"Now," I say to Mel, "do you trust me?"

"Yes," Mel says, squaring her shoulders. "I trust you."

"First rule," I say, grabbing the laptop case off the bed. "No matter what, we don't get upset. No matter what your mom says. We have to show her we're mature."

"Right," Mel says. She's wearing her gray dress, and even though she has a nervous look on her face, she looks really pretty.

We march downstairs to where Mel's mom is sitting at the kitchen table. Mel told her we were going to be doing a special presentation for her. And then she made her up a cheese and crackers plate to snack on while we changed into our secretary clothes.

"Good afternoon," I say. "And welcome to our presentation."

I open my dad's computer, and boot it up. "This afternoon, I will be presenting you with reasons why it doesn't make sense to send Mel to a private school." I flip open the computer, and double click on the PowerPoint presentation icon on the desktop. Navy blue fills the screen, and white letters show the words

"Private School vs. Public School." Then, in small letters underneath, it says, "What they don't want you to know." My dad thought that was taking it a little bit too far, but I thought it had to have some kind of hook, you know, like a *Dateline* special or something. Otherwise it just doesn't have the same impact.

"'What they don't want you to know?'" Mel's mom asks uncertainly.

"Yes," I say seriously. "'They' being the private schools." I try to make my voice sounds just a touch ominous, since this is a very serious situation going on here.

"Let's please turn our attention to slide number one," I say, "which shows us that in a recent study conducted by the National Center for Education Statistics, children who went to private schools only outperformed children in public schools in eighth grade reading. That's a comprehensive study of every child in every grade, in every subject." I pause. "And as we all know, Mel is ahead of her grade level in reading, and has been since, like, kindergarten. So she wouldn't benefit from this." I clear my throat and remind myself that serious researchers probably don't say "like." Although they totally should. Some of this data is pretty boring, and it could probably use a little bit of lightening up.

Mel's mom doesn't look that convinced. "Anyone can manufacture data," she says.

"Let's look at a study from an independent research firm," I say. I turn to the second slide, this one a graph of a study that showed students who went to private school had no real advantage when it came to getting into college. "This slide shows that the most important factor in a student gaining admission to college is grades. The second most important factor is if the student has a parent who went to that school."

Mel's mom raises her eyebrows at this, and I can tell I have her a little bit interested.

"And," I say, quickly moving to the next slide. "There has also been research showing that school uniforms actually *stifle* a student's creativity." I try to say "stifle" in a really shocked voice, like getting your creativity stifled is the most horrible thing that can happen to you. The slide I made is a picture of Mel in a school uniform that I Photoshopped on, and next to her is a picture of a rock crushing the word "creativity." Mel's mom gives a little smile at this one.

I go on to show how yanking someone out of their school environment can cause undue stress and cause a person's grades to go down, and how our school district has some of the best teachers and the best standardized test scores in the state. I show how public schools lend students a better, diverse experience when it comes to socialization, and how these social skills can benefit them throughout college and beyond. I follow everything up with a list of famous smart people who went to public school, and a list of politicians who chose to send their children to public school, like President Carter, who sent his daughter Amy to public school while he was in office.

"Thank you for your time," I say when it's all over. And then I add something that my dad told me to do, just in case Mel's mom might think I'm coming into her house and telling her how to raise her daughter. "Of course, I just want what's best for Mel, and I understand that the decision lies in your hands, and so I'm sorry if I've stepped on any toes. I just thought we'd present our case in a better way than, uh, bringing Corbin over here."

"That was a very impressive presentation, girls," Mel's mom says, sighing. She grips the coffee mug she's holding tighter and looks at us over her reading glasses. "But it still doesn't change the fact that you lied to me last weekend."

"I know," I say. "And I'm sorry. But we all know that under normal circumstances, Mel would never,

ever do something like that. She's the most honest girl I know." This is true. Mel hates lying. She's the one who was always urging me to just be honest with Luke, and to confront my dad about the whole affair thing. "So she must have been under real duress to do something like that."

Mel's mom bites her lip and sighs. "You really, really don't want to go to private school, huh?"

"I really, really don't want to," Mel says. "All my friends are here. I like my school, I like my teachers." She looks down at her hands. "My grades are good."

"That is true," Mel's mom says. "Your grades are good."

"Maybe we could make a deal," Mel says. "As long as my grades stay good, I get to stay?"

Mel's mom doesn't say anything at first, and I hold my breath. Then she turns to me, turns to Mel, and sighs. "Okay," she says. "If you really, really, don't want to go, then you can stay at your school."

Mel and I yell and scream and jump up and down. Which is very hard to do in the heels that I'm wearing, FYI.

"If," Mel's mom says as we both hug her, "if you keep your grades up."

"Thanks, Mom," Mel says. She hugs her again, and

as she looks over her shoulder, there's a little bit of a tear in her eye as she mouths to me, *And thank you, too.*

"You're welcome," I say, smiling back.

Two hours later, I am sitting on the bus to go over to the mock trial competition, and I am sooo happy. I don't even care that this is going to be totally not fun. I don't even care that I'm going to be seeing Luke. I don't even care that I forgot to change out of my secretary clothes and now I look like I got dressed up to go watch a mock trial competition. Mel isn't going to private school! I cannot stop smiling.

Well. Until Kim Cavalli sits down next to me. You'd think that she would be sitting with Bailey Barelli, since those two are BFF. You'd *think.* But in an even worse twist, Bailey is sitting with Luke. The only thing I can comfort myself with is the fact that it seemed like this was orchestrated more by her than by Luke.

When I got on the bus, Luke was already sitting in one of the seats about halfway back, looking out the window. He didn't look up when I passed by, but then Bailey got on the bus and was all, "Oh, Luke! I've totally been meaning to talk to you about something!" and then she plopped down right next to him. And then Kim got on the bus and sat down next to *me,* and she's been blabbing away for the past ten minutes.

It's actually very annoying. She keeps trying to act like she's being nice, when she's really not. For example, she says things like, "I'm so glad that you and Lexi are still friends, I mean, nobody thought you guys would ever patch it up after you lied to her and then tried to keep her and Jared apart."

The only good thing about sitting with Kim is that she said she thought it was fabulous that I was back with Greg, which means that Luke didn't tell Bailey that I made that up. I'm not sure what that means. That he wanted to be nice because he still likes me? That he thinks I'm pathetic? That he doesn't care and so it just didn't cross his mind? That he hasn't talked to Bailey since last night?

By the time I get off the bus, my head is spinning around and around and around. Mr. Ikwang is so excited I'm afraid he might pass out or something.

"Students, students," he says as he herds us into Westland High, where the competition is going to be taking place. "Everyone into the auditorium, please, that's it, that's it, take your seats."

The auditorium is mostly filled with parents of the kids that are going to be putting on the mock trial. I get stuck sitting next to Kim, with Luke and Bailey sitting a couple of rows ahead of us and a few seats over. Ugh. I can't decide what's worse—being able to see what they're doing, or not being able to see what they're doing.

"I'm just so glad that Lexi and Jared are together," Kim is saying. "And I don't know why she hates me so much. I mean, it would be so much easier for everyone at our lunch table if we could just get along, you know?"

"Yeah," I say, not really listening. And then the mock trial competition starts. It's a case in which two kids hacked into some computer system and made the alarms at a zoo go all wonky. It should be an interesting case, but I can't keep my mind on it.

I keep watching as Bailey leans over and whispers things to Luke. What is she saying? What is he saying back? Does he like her still? Is he even thinking about me?

Kim spends the whole time keeping up her super annoying chatter by whispering to me every second, everything from how the people in mock trial are dressed ("Ohmigod, can you believe she's wearing those shoes?") to how crazy Mr. Ikwang is ("Check out his face, could he be liking this any more?") to finally remarking on me staring at Luke ("You don't still like him, do you? Won't Greg be jealous?").

When the mock trial competition is finally over, I'm relieved. I can't believe I made it through without killing myself. And as we file out of the gym and back onto the bus, I make a decision. No more mock trial. It's ridiculous to join something because the guy you like is in it. Me being in mock trial didn't make Luke like me more. All it did was cause me to make up a fake boyfriend who ended up making Luke like me *less*. And to stay in mock trial just so I can keep an eye on Luke and Bailey is just dumb. I should be in radio with Mel and Lexi, like I want to. I feel a little cheered, thinking that after today, I won't have to listen to any more fake trials.

"Now," Mr. Ikwang says. "How did everyone like their first mock trial competition?"

Everyone sort of stares at each other blankly. Honestly, teachers shouldn't ask questions like this. No one's going to offer how much they liked something that's, let's face it, a little bit nerdy.

"Anyone?" Mr. Ikwang says. "Bailey, what did you think?"

"Personally, I loved it," Bailey says. So much for the theory about people not wanting to admit they liked something so nerdy. "I know we weren't sup- posed to be talking during it, but Luke and I couldn't help remarking on how impressed we were seeing the trials come to life."

Ugh. Luke and I? I slip down further in my seat, wondering how long we're going to stay here talking about this. Maybe I should raise my hand and let Mr. Ikwang know I need to be home immediately. Like for a family birthday party or something. Mr. Ikwang asks a few more questions, and kids raise their hands to answer them. *Come on,* I'm thinking. *I want to get out of here.*

"Devon?" Mr. Ikwang asks. "What did you think of the case?"

Um, I dunno because I wasn't paying attention, since I was too busy spying on my ex-boyfriend and his ex-girlfriend? "I liked it," I say, hoping that will suffice. Then I pull my binder out of my book bag and pretend that I'm taking notes. This is a trick I used to use last year in science when I didn't want to be called on. I'd pretend I was taking notes on something, and usually that would work.

"What did you like about it?" Mr. Ikwang persists.

"Well," I say slowly. Everyone has turned to look at me now, and I can see Bailey out of the corner of my eye. I can't be sure, but I swear she's smirking at me. "I liked that it was kind of hard to tell if the person was guilty or not." This seems safe, because hello? If the cases weren't controversial, we wouldn't be doing them in mock trial.

I shoot Bailey a smirk right back, and notice that Luke isn't looking at me. Of course not.

"And what was your personal opinion on it?" Mr. Ikwang wants to know.

"I think that what happened was something that just sort of got out of control," I say, looking down at my hands. "I don't think those kids really wanted anything bad to happen, but they started something, and it was too late to stop. I think they're really sorry, and that everyone deserves a second chance." For some reason, my voice catches in my throat at that last part, but it's only for a second, and then it passes.

Mr. Ikwang moves on, and after a couple more questions, the bus driver starts the bus, and we're on our way home. Thank God. I cannot wait to get home, maybe take a bubble bath, and call Mel to celebrate the fact that she's not going to private school and finally get the dirt on her and Dylan. And then maybe I'll cheer myself up by getting online and planning out the color scheme for my room in the new house.

"That was sooo boring," Kim's saying from the seat

next to me. I tried to ditch her in the crowd on the way out of the school, but she's like gum in my hair—I cannot get rid of her.

"Yeah," I say, pulling my iPod out of my bag.

Kim doesn't get the hint. "God, I mean, I only joined this because Bailey wanted me to, and it's, like, such a waste of time." She reaches into her bag and pulls a brush out, then slides it through her hair. "Sooo boring. At least we're not getting graded on stuff."

I slide the earbuds into my ears. "Yeah," I say. And then someone taps me on the shoulder from the seat behind me. Sigh. I look up, and hanging over the seat is Luke. His face is like one inch away from mine.

"Oh," I say, turning around to face him and hastily pulling the buds out of my ears. "Hi."

"Hey," he says softly.

"Hey!" Kim says brightly. "I thought you were sitting up there with Bailey?"

"Um, can I talk to you for a second?" Luke asks, ignoring Kim.

"Sure," I say. "What's up?" My heart is beating so loud in my chest that I'm afraid Kim will be able to hear the vibrations.

"I can't stop thinking about what happened last night," he says. His lips are so close to mine that for a second, I think he might kiss me, right there on the bus in front of everyone.

"Why?" Kim asks loudly, looking between me and Luke. "What happened last night?"

"Can we switch seats, please?" Luke asks. And before Kim can answer, he's standing in the aisle in front of our seat. Kim has no choice but to move. And as they switch places, I catch a look at Bailey's face from a few seats ahead of us, looking back, totally shocked.

"Look," Luke says, sliding in next to me. "I'm sorry I didn't call you. That wasn't nice of me."

"It's fine," I say. I turn away and look toward the window, but Luke puts his hand on my shoulder and I turn back around. He leans in close to me, resting his head on the back of the seat in front of us.

"I didn't know you made Greg up," he says. "And when I saw you at the mall with him that day, I realized how much I liked you, and I guess I didn't know how to handle it."

"I know," I say. I look down at my hands and play with the clasp of the silver chain bracelet I'm wearing. "And I'm sorry I lied. It's just that Bailey kept talking about all that four-wheeling, and then she ate some of your pizza."

He looks confused. "My pizza?"

"Yeah, that day in the cafeteria, and I dunno, I just . . ." I take a deep breath and decide to go for the truth. "I thought you might still like her."

"Devon," he says, reaching over and taking my hand. "I like *you*. Not Bailey. Not some girl who has a crazy ex-boyfriend named Greg. *You*. The real you. The girl I saw last night, the one who was waiting for her dad and just being herself."

"You do?"

"Yes," he says, smiling. "And I still want to be your boyfriend. If you can forgive me for ignoring you like that."

"I think I can," I say, smiling. Ohmigod, ohmigod, ohmigod! Luke and I are back together. It's all I can do not to stand up and shout it at Barelli and everyone else.

"But, um, Luke?" I say. "I have one more confession to make."

"Oh, yeah," he says, looking a little nervous. "What's that?"

"I hate mock trial."

Luke bursts out laughing. We talk for the rest of the ride, and when we pull up in front of our school, Luke takes my hand as we walk toward my mom's car. Right past Barelli, who has a totally scandalized look on her face.

"I'll text you later," Luke says. And then he kisses my cheek.

I can see my mom through the windshield, her mouth gaping. And I smile and head toward the car. Ready to let my mom know that yes, I hold hands with my boyfriend, and sometimes he even kisses me. Ready to figure out this whole moving thing. Ready to go home. Ready to be the real Devon Delaney.

I get into the car, and Katie's sleeping in the backseat.

"Who's there?" she asks groggily, stirring on the seat.

I smile. "It's just me." And finally, that's enough.